THE SPACE PIONEER
SUNITA WILLIAMS
A COMPLETE BIOGRAPHY

THE SPACE PIONEER

SUNITA WILLIAMS

A COMPLETE BIOGRAPHY

PALLAVI BORGOHAIN

Published by
PRABHAT PRAKASHAN PVT. LTD.
4/19 Asaf Ali Road,
New Delhi-110 002 (INDIA)
e-mail: prabhatbooks@gmail.com

ISBN 978-93-5562-449-9

SUNITA WILLIAMS: A COMPLETE BIOGRAPHY
by Pallavi Borgohain

Edition
2025

Price
₹ 350 (Rupees Three Hundred Fifty Only)

Printed at
Sita Fine Arts, Delhi

Author's Note

An Ordinary But Extraordinary in its Own Way...

Sunita Williams needs no special introduction - an icon of courage and endurance - her extraordinary capabilities embodies the modern woman. The dedicated and determined—that is how we can describe her. The beauty blended with brain, Sunita Williams had acquired those accolades which every woman feel envious of. Her space odysseys speak volumes of her courage and conviction.

Soaring above the skies, Sunita Williams is the second woman of Indian roots after Kalpana Chawla who was selected by NASA for a space mission. Kalpana Chawla made two shuttle flights, the first aboard Columbia in 1997. Her second flight, also aboard Columbia, ended in tragedy when the shuttle broke up during re-entry on February 1, 2003. Sunita holds three world records for female space travellers thus far. She has held the undisputed record for the longest space flight, which stands at 195 days, four spacewalks—the highest for a female astronaut till date and also for the highest total number of time spent on space walks (29 hours and 17 minutes).

She was exceptional...Her passion was unlike womanly or feminine interests but something daring and difficult. She attempted to achieve the exceptional. Sunita Williams once said, "Don't let anyone tell you, 'You can't do it'. That's the biggest thing — I had one squad commander [tell me]: 'Being an astronaut is for jet pilots, not for helicopter pilots'. If you know that's what you want, you've just got to go for it. You do the best you can do at what you're doing, and find out what you need to do to get into this field'.

According to her father, Sunita has always been the adventurous type. After her induction into NASA in June 1998, she had to undergo rigorous orientation briefing, shuttle system and flight training and survival techniques to meet the requirements of an astronaut candidate. Sunita became a helicopter pilot. She served in the Mediterranean, Red Sea, and Persian Gulf in support of Desert Shield. In 1993, she graduated from the US Naval Test Pilot School, and went on to perform test flights in various military helicopters. In 1995, she completed her Master's degree in Engineering Management. Her turning point in life was her decision to join the US Naval Academy as advised by her brother. She decided to follow in his footsteps. Later in 1987 she graduated from the academy with a Bachelor of Science degree in Physical Science.

Like every child, Sunita Williams too had her own dreams. She wanted to become a "Vet", but ended up becoming an astronaut.

Manmohan Singh, the former Prime Minister of India has hailed Sunita as an inspiration to all women whose dreams know no limit.

❑

Contents

Where I Began

The Blooming Bud.....

September 19, 1965. It was the luckiest day for the Indian American neuro anatomist Deepak Pandya and Slovene American Ursuline Bonnie Pandya (née Zalokar), as they were blessed with a multi-talented angel, Sunita Williams. The youngest of three children, Sunita Williams was born in Euclid, Ohio. Her brother Jay Thomas is four years older and her sister Dina Anna is three years older.

Sunita's parents were a residents of Falmouth, Massachusetts. Williams' paternal ancestry is from Jhulasan, Mehsana district in Gujarat, India. Her mother said, right after Sunita Williams' birth they moved to Boston, Massahausetts, so that Deepak Pandya could continue his research work which he had started at the Case-Western Reserve Institute in Cleveland.

Family

The Pandya family loved adventures. Deepak and Bonnie along with the three children Jay, Dina and Suni are embodiments of perfect family bonding. They reflected a perfect blend of west and east. They inculcated among their children both western and Indian ideologies.

The family enjoyed every aspect of life. Deepak Pandya was a busy doctor and researcher but despite that he ensured he gave quality time to the family. Weekends were pakora and Sukhadi days where Deepak Pandya would cook for the family. So would Bonnie try her culinary skills in Gujarati dishes.

They are liberal in their religious views too. Bonnie was a Catholic and Deepak Pandya an ardent follower of Hinduism. Every Sunday the family would go to Church and Deepak would carry the Bhagavad Gita along with him.

They are liberal in their religious views too. Bonnie was a Catholic and Deepak Pandya an ardent follower of Hinduism. Every Sunday the family would go to Church and Deepak would carry the *Bhagavad Gita* along with him. Often, their house remained the meeting place of several learned Swamis coming from India. The Pandya family hosted the Swamis and the children got the opportunities to acknowledge themselves with valuable discussions pertaining to religion, spirituality, God and science.

Despite his busy schedule, Deepak spent time with his children. He told his children stories from the Ramayana, Mahabharata, Nal Damayanti and other folk tales of India.

It was as if he tried to establish a missing link between the generations and his roots. He recalls his childhood days when his mother told him bed time stories of Rama and Sita, and other legendary and mythological heroes. Often Suni, Dina and Jay asked to repeat those episodes of the Ramayana when Lakshmana cut Suparnakha's nose, and Hanuman bringing sanjivani. Also they enjoyed listening to the acts of Arjuna and the story of Karna in the Mahabharata.

It was Sunita's wedding at St Joseph's Church, Woods Hole, Cape Cod. This church has a long ancient history and is known to have the oldest Mary Garden. On this day many friends and relatives from India, Slovenia, Russia, US and Australia were a part of the auspicious celebrations.

For the Pandyas Christmas and Diwali were important days. They celebrated these festivals with great enthusiasm.

The Pandyas loved adventure. Early at five Bonnie would warm up her Ford station wagon and wait for her children to get into the car. Though Suni was the youngest of the three, she never came late to join them. Their mother would drive them to the swimming pool at Havard University where they enjoyed swimming every day.

Tying the Knot.....

Her father Deepak Pandya recollects, "I distinctly remember that fine sunny day of her wedding. All the flowers bloomed with jubilant flavour, colour and fragrance and all the birds sang with joy".

It was Sunita's wedding at St Joseph's Church, Woods Hole, Cape Cod. This church has a long ancient history and is known to have the oldest Mary Garden. On this day many friends and relatives from India, Slovenia, Russia, US and Australia were a part of the auspicious celebrations. She got married in the year 1989.

Of course it was the wedding of a special one. People around were cheerful. So who was the groom? The lucky one who was able to seal the heart of this multi-talented bride was none other than one of her batch mates at the Naval Academy, the young and energetic Michael Williams.

Michael and Sunita moved towards their own dreams right after the completion of graduation. They lost touch with each other after leaving USNA. It was only after several years that Sunita came across Michael at a friend's wedding at Pensacola, Florida. Their memories renewed and both of them spent the whole day together. They loved each other's company so much that they just felt that they needed to catch up again. They shared their experiences, life and they had so many things to share that they soon came to realise that they person actually meant for each other.

They dated for two years after their meeting at the wedding of their friend at Pensacola. Sunita describes Michael to be a very straightforward person and trustworthy. She calls him a dependable person. Towards the end of their flight school they decided to get married. The wedding was a grand affair in the presence of friends and relatives from several countries, including India and Slovenia, the countries of her parents.

"I got married in Woods Hole", said Williams. St Joseph's Church had a long history of having the oldest Mary garden. Sunita wore a white gown and Michael with his stripes looked a handsome Navy officer from all angles.

❑

My Roots Define Me

Sunita Williams' father Deepak Pandya recollects, "I was born in Mangrol, a tiny town situated in the west coast of Saurashtra in India. I was born on 6 December, 1932 to a business family who run their family business at Bombay (Now Mumbai)". His father died when Deepak Pandya was only two years old. He met with his other tragedy when his mother also died when he was just thirteen years old. He began his early education in Julhason village in North Gujarat and later on continued his studies in Ahmedabad.

Out of sheer perseverance and dedication, Deepak Pandya established himself as a competent doctor after completing his professional studies at Surat in 1957. He worked in V.C. Hospital as an intern. After his parents it was Navin, this elder brother who inspired him. He followed in his footsteps and headed to United States, at a time in the late 1950s, when air travel was not in vogue. He started his journey to the USA in a ship. Bonnie recollects, "I started from Jhulasan to Mumbai by train, from there by ship to London and after reaching there I boarded "The Queen Elizabeth", another ship to New York. It took me twenty-one days to get there".

His destination was Euclid where Dr. Deepak Pandya joined the Euclid General hospital. Being a dedicated medico, Deepak Pandya excelled in his profession. He completed his internship and residency training in medicine at the Euclid General Hospital, Ohio.

The memories of the journey are still vivid in Deepak Pandya's mind. He says, "I was not fluent in English". But he had to talk to many people on the ship in English. By the time he reached his destination he was very confident about speaking in English.

His destination was Euclid where Dr. Deepak Pandya joined the Euclid General hospital. Being a dedicated medico, Deepak Pandya excelled in his profession. He completed his internship and residency training in medicine at the Euclid General Hospital, Ohio. As he started from home he thought he would return to India and practise his profession in the motherland. But destiny unfolded some pleasant surprises.

Often in the hospital cafeteria he came across a young X-Ray technician who not only stole his glances but also his heart. He never dared to talk to her till he was introduced to her at a night party later. Her name was Bonnie. This brief introduction became a lifelong commitment. They started dating each other – spent hours being together, and that is how time flew. And after six months the two youngsters committed for a life together. They tied the note in a church in the presence of a few friends and relatives. The couple is blessed with three children Jay, Dina and Suni (Sunita Williams). Jay was born in 1961, Dina in 1962 and Sunita in the year 1965. The children are named by their aunt Neelam and often a Gujarati name was selected to keep their roots alive.

His soul mate Bonnie Ursaline Zalokar, proud mother of the reputed astronaut Sunita Williams, recalls about how it all happened. She recollects, "I had a scholarship to study music but I decided to go to X-Ray Technician School at the Euclid General Hospital. It is where I meet Deepak".

Things changed, the two years in the US passed and thus his decision to come back to India remained just a thought. Deepak continued his residency training in neurology at the Case Western University. Thus his professional journey headed towards new horizons in America. He became an American citizen, a year before Sunita was born. He taught at prestigious institutions like the Harvard Medical School and Boston University Medical School and worked at several hospitals in and around Boston. Here after the family started living in Boston—the hub of education and medicine on the east coast of America.

His soul mate Bonnie Ursaline Zalokar, proud mother of the reputed astronaut Sunita Williams, recalls about how it all happened. She recollects, "I had a scholarship to study music but I decided to go to X-Ray Technician School at the Euclid General Hospital. It is where I meet Deepak".

Perhaps destiny had different plans. Deepak was a resident physician at this hospital and that is where Bonnie too came for her studies. It is where they met each other and got married.

Her mother was a Slovene emigrant. Her maternal great-grandmother Mary Bohinc (originally Marija Bohinjec), born on September 5, 1890 in Leše, Slovenia emigrated to America as an eleven-year-old girl with her mother, an 1891 Slovene emigrant Ursula Bohinc née Strajhar. However, Bonnie's parents were born in Cleveland, Ohio. Bonnie was also born and brought up at Cleveland, Ohio, where the Zalokar family ran their family business.

Her grandfather and father owned a delicatessen and a shop selling ready-to-eat food products. Bonnie belonged to a respectable family. They are highly regarded among the Slovenian community. Bonnie had six maternal aunts and her father's family had three girls and four boys. The lived a happy-go-lucky life. The families enjoyed weekends together with good music, games and home made Slovenian food.

Sunni's mother had two brothers and a sister. Bonnie's sister was a teacher and her brother Tony worked as a marine in Vietnam. The other one Hank retired from General Motors, a big American corporation. Her brother Tony died at the age of thirty-three in a road accident.

Bonnie had excellent culinary skills inherited from her family. She tried her skills in vegetarian Gujarati dishes. The most interesting fact was that every meal in the Pandya family was a mosaic of American and Indian food. Bonnie loved baking and that's how her girls started to develop interests in baking.

Bonnie was a music aficionado, and so was the whole family. All of them played one or the other musical instrument. Her brother Tony had a good hand at guitar and brother Hank loved to spend time with his favourite instrument the saxophone and the clarinet. Mother was also good at piano and her father was a banjo lover. Her sister played the piano and she in the accordion - all together enjoyed performing music. Often they enjoyed themselves as a family band.

❑

The Initial Steps

Schooling at Needham

Sunita began her regular schooling at Hillside Elementary School, Needham where she studied from kindergarten till sixth grade. And thereafter she joined Newman Junior High School to study from the seventh till ninth grade. She did her tenth and twelfth from Needham High School. Williams graduated from Needham High School in Needham, Massachusetts, in 1983.

Sunita loved science. Her interest was complemented by her favourite teacher Angela Di Napoli. Her sixth grade science was at her fingertips. So was the seventh grade science where Mr. Perkins made learning science great fun and most enjoyable. On the other hand, Ms, Piotrowski encouraged the students in gardening. She had some real life experience in

Marine biology when her teacher Mr. Tomkowitz took her to Cape Cod on a research trip. All these mentors directly or indirectly increased her love for science. Her father's contribution was also immense. Being a neuroscientist he greatly influenced his daughter's interests.

The Pandya family became a paradise for the children of the neighbourhood with lovely pets. Sunita too became a great pet lover and her desire to become a veterinary doctor grew strong every day. She thought that an animal doctor was her perfect career choice.

However, Sunita was more inclined towards veterinary science. Her parents also thought that she would become a vet. Bonnie Pandya was very fond of dogs. When Sunita was five years old the family bought their first dog, Lassie. Lassie had a litter and the family kept one. They named it Banjo combining the initial alphabets of Bonnie and her mother Josephine. So the number of pets increased in number year after year. The Pandya family became a paradise for the children of the neighbourhood with lovely pets. Sunita too became a great pet lover and her desire to become a veterinary doctor grew strong every day. She thought that an animal doctor was her perfect career choice. After her graduation at Needham School, she looked forward to her career.

"I wasn't a triple A student. I failed two college courses. But I learned from the failure", says Ms. Williams, of both Indian and Slovenian descent in one of her visits to India.

She put in applications for getting enrolled in the college. One among her choice was the reputed Columbia University.

Her sister Dina was already in Smith College, in Massachusetts and her brother at the US Naval Academy (USNA).

> In those days the application to the USNA had to be endorsed by a Congress man and the Massachussets senator was Edward Kennedy. Her application impressed the senator because she was multi-skilled - an athlete, swimmer and a girl of immense enthusiasm. A promising future was waiting for her.

It was time of Jay's graduation and the family visited Maryland where Jay proudly showed them the USNA campus. Her brother thought that it would be a perfect place for his sister Sunita who was multi-talented and had an inclination for athletics. Jay told her about his experiences of heading the swimming team of the academy. Sunita was passionate about swimming too. So, when Jay narrated his experience she was enchanted by the beautiful campus and the exciting experiences, he shared. She was tempted but at the same time was scared that she might have to lose her long cherished dream of becoming a vet. It would mean losing her long hair and so many other favourite things as there are some rules for the Naval Academy. However when she gave it a serious thought that she started to dream about becoming the one among the few women that became naval officers. It was in the year of Jay's graduation the first batch of women graduated from the Academy. Women in the armed forces were still a long distant dream. She was confused and was not very willing to give up her dream but at the same time she felt tempted to explore greener pastures. After all the analysis she decided to follow in her brother's footsteps. Her life took a profound turn.

She applied for the Academy. In those days the application to the USNA had to be endorsed by a Congress man and the Massachussets senator was Edward Kennedy. Her application impressed the senator because she was multi-skilled - an athlete, swimmer and a girl of immense enthusiasm. A promising future was waiting for her. Her application was accepted and she got admission in the Academy in the year 1983.

Glorious Four Years in the USNA

A new Sunita among a group of a hundred others—a girl with navy cut hair and a girl full of energy. So, the journey began. She ended up at the Naval Academy, not because she had always planned to study there, but because she was looking for an affordable college education.

Life in the Academy was not a bed of roses. The first six weeks is the toughest time that every student undergoes before actually beginning the real academics. It is more of a transition from civilian to military life. Every year more than thousand plebes enter the academy who are then grouped into fifteen companies made up of two platoons each which comprises four squads of ten plebes each. The squads work together as a team initially during the summer. Later, by the end of the summer these plebes are sworn into the Navy as midshipmen. It was the toughest period in the Academy.

For Sunita life at the Academy was enjoyable. She could impress the people around by her swimming skills. During the plebe summer she won wide acclamation as an athlete. She also got adorned with an award for endurance. She accepted the challenges positively and felt that she was in the right place to manifest her swimming skills that she acquired after years of compromising sweet dawn sleep for the swimming practice. She felt that being in the Academy was something more than being at the Smith College where Dina, her sister studied.

As the tradition of USNA, every year as a part of the year-end festivities, the Herndon Monument is covered with lard. And the custom is that the plebes climbed the monument to remove a 'Dixie Cup' and put a hat on the top. Dixie cup is the traditional cap that the plebes wore.

"Morning shows the day", so the saying goes. During the plebe days itself her talents can be assumed. It was customary to climb the Herndon monument located in the Academy by the plebes to mark the successful completion of the first year. As the tradition of USNA, every year as a part of the year-end festivities, the Herndon Monument is covered with lard. And the custom is that the plebes climbed the monument to remove a 'Dixie Cup' and put a hat on the top. Dixie cup is the traditional cap that the plebes wore. This marks the successful completion of the first year. Sunita was the only woman who climbed the greased monument. Her friends cheered her and by the time she got half way up they pulled her back. It was all out of fellow feeling.

The spirit of camaraderie was evident among the fellow students of the Academy. Her close friends included Michael J. Williams (her husband), Debbie Klatt, Vicky Webster, Ron Harris and Heidi Miser. Ron Harris is presently the

Director of Athletics at the USNA and a world class runner. He organised a number of people from Maryland to run the Boston Marathon and also help Dina and Suni participate in the run. Years after, when Suni went into space he had his students make a plaque for Sunita and supported her as Suni's Earth Support team. Their friendship remained lifelong. At her wedding her roommates Heidi, Debie and Vicky became bridesmaids and they supported each other throughout their stay in the Academy. During those days very few women joined the Academy.

Later on three of her friends surprised her by visiting her on her fortieth birthday at Cape Cod.

> So there I was at the Naval Academy with shorter hair and learning how to march, it was a little bit of a surprise for me but I blended in pretty quickly and I really had fun and I learned fellowship going through the ranks there, and teamwork. I was on the Swim team there; I was on the cross-country team, on the bike club, so a lot of sports, like my brother suggested.

Her days became more challenging because the Academy was preparing the students for military life. Sunita was always an adventure lover. She loved and coped very well with the atmosphere. She recollects", So there I was at the Naval Academy with shorter hair and learning how to march, it was a little bit of a surprise for me but I blended in pretty quickly and I really had fun and I learned fellowship going through the ranks there, and teamwork. I was on the Swim team there; I was on the cross-country team, on the bike club, so a lot of sports, like my brother suggested. I went to jump schools and stuff like that, just a lot of good outdoor stuff…."

Sunita excelled in all she opted for and coped well with academics as well as extra curricular activities successfully. She was diligent and at the same time talented. Like all teens she managed her time well and that is how she cleared her academics in the Academy. Once she reached the second year the students had to choose one of the subjects as a Major. Sunita opted for Naval Architecture but after some time she realised that she was unable to handle all the activities as well as her academics smoothly. Therefore she opted for General Sciences and withdrew from Naval Architecture. Sunita graduated from the Academy in 1987.

Sunita says, "I was not a class topper and my achievements are nevertheless significant". However, she successfully participated in every event of the Academy. Like her elder brother Jay and sister Dina she took responsibilities as a captain of various sports teams, including the cross-country team, swimming team and the biking team. After graduation and putting on the rank of ensign, she had three choices in hand to enter the surface line—Navy Air, Marine and Submarine services. Swimming being her favourite so she applied for the Navy Diving but to her disappointment she was not offered the choice—the single vacancy that existed at that time. And for the second time in life she had to miss her first choice again and she applied for the Navy Air. She had no option but to love the option God had assigned for her. In a way it was the first step of the ladder leading to the destination—an astronaut.

Surprises, twists and turns are always on her way. Before her air training began she got an opportunity to spend some six months time in diving. She worked head over heels to get a Basic Diving Officer Certificate. After the completion of the six month diving classes she reported at the Naval Aviation Training Command to begin her training to fly. Destiny always played tricks. Once again she had to compromise with her choice. Ideally she was all set to fly a combat aircraft byt she had to opt for a helicopter. She recollects," It was the time of Top Gun, so I wanted to be a jet pilot. That did not materialise either. I became a helicopter pilot. But I found that I really loved flying helicopters. I loved working on helicopters. I appreciate the crew concept and team work with the crewman in the back."

Sunita was an enthusiastic learner. She learned everything that came her way very sincerely. She became passionate about helicopters. Very soon her passion for swimming was overshadowed by her love for flying. She emerged as an excellent helicopter flier.

❑

Climbing the Ladder

Dreams and reality never coincide. Sunita always wanted to become a vet and so her parents thought. After graduation at Needham High School, she joined the US Naval Academy. Her entry to the US Naval Academy was the turning point of her life.

Military Career

Sunita after completing her studies in physical sciences in the US Naval Academy at Annapolis, Maryland started her military career.

She joined the military in a time of peace. In August 1991, Saddam Hussein invaded Kuwait. She was on a ship in the Mediterranean. "It's sort of funny, kind of like a switch turned. We were going from port to port – France, Spain, good food, all relaxing to all of a sudden battle groups pulling through the Mediterranean and we are up all night," recalled Williams. "The war paint came out, which was a bit shocking but it made people have a purpose for our job. It made more of a team for the whole military." One year later, Hurricane Andrew hit Miami, giving justification to "one of the whole reasons I wanted to be a helicopter pilot," said Williams. She was in the office of helicopter detachment bringing supplies, food and water, to neighbourhoods. "We would take multiple runs. We were landing in baseball fields, stuff like that" she said.

She received a Bachelor of Science degree in physical science from the United States Naval Academy in 1987. After a six-month temporary assignment at the Naval Coastal System Command, she was designated a Basic Diving Officer. She next reported to the Naval Air Training Command, where she was designated a Naval Aviator in July 1989.

She received a Bachelor of Science degree in physical science from the United States Naval Academy in 1987. After a six-month temporary assignment at the Naval Coastal System Command, she was designated a Basic Diving Officer. She next reported to the Naval Air Training Command, where she was designated a Naval Aviator in July 1989. She received the initial H-46 Sea Knight training in Helicopter Combat Support Squadron 3 (HC-3), and was then assigned to Helicopter Combat Support Squadron 8 (HC-8) in Norfolk, Virginia, with which she made overseas deployments to the Mediterranean, Red Sea and the Persian Gulf for Operation Desert Shield and Operation Provide Comfort. In July 1989 she began combat helicopter training. She flew in helicopter support squadrons during the preparations for the Persian Gulf War and the establishment of no-fly zones over Kurdish areas of Iraq, as well as in relief missions during Hurricane Andrew in 1992 in Miami. She was the officer-in charge of a H46 detachment sent to Miami for Hurricane relief operations on board the USS Sylvania.

Williams was deployed on Saipan in June 1998 when she was selected by NASA for the astronaut programme. After flying three different aircraft in one day at test pilot school, "I went home at night and had a beer and thought, that was a pretty cool day." - Sunita Williams.

Aviator...Test Pilot and So On

In January 1993, she was selected for the United States Naval Test Pilot School and after completion of the course she became a naval test pilot. In December 1993, she graduated from the US Naval Test Pilot School, and went on to perform test flights in a variety of military helicopters. She was assigned with the Rotary wing Aircraft Test Directorate as an H46 Project Officer, and V-22 Chase pilot in the T-2.

In January 1993, Williams began training at the US Naval Test Pilot School. She graduated in December, and was assigned to the Rotary Wing Aircraft Test Directorate as an H-46 Project Officer and V-22 chase pilot in the T-2. In December 1995, she went back to the Naval Test Pilot School as an instructor in the Rotary Wing Department and as the school's Safety Officer. There she flew the UH-60,OH-6, and the OH-58. She was then assigned to USS Saipan as the

Aircraft Handler and the Assistant Air Boss. Williams was deployed on Saipan in June 1998 when she was selected by NASA for the astronaut programme.

After flying three different aircraft in one day at test pilot school, "I went home at night and had a beer and thought, that was a pretty cool day." – Sunita Williams. She had the leadership responsibility of getting people to work together. "It's terribly rewarding," she said.

> Now Sunita was keen to be an astronaut. She researched on how it could be possible and applied for her Master's degree. She was deployed on board the USS Saipan when she was selected for the astronaut programme. She logged more than 2000 flight hours in about 30 aircrafts.

While the work was rewarding, a constant theme in her journey has been the quest to learn more. She liked working with maintenance and working on engines, so she applied to be a test pilot to learn more about how safety procedures are developed. She also had a chance to learn about many types of aircraft. She was a helicopter pilot but "we all get to fly everything at some point in time," she said. Williams has flown more than 30 aircraft. The three types of test pilots are jet pilots, helicopter pilots and prop pilots, she said. Thereafter she worked in various positions and assignments, including a test pilot instructor. She flew more than 30 different aircraft and logged more than 2,770 flight hours. Being a helicopter pilot she served in the Mediterranean, Red Sea, and Persian Gulf in support of Desert Shield.

During her field trips she often visited the Johnson Space Centre, Houston, Texas. During her classes she came across veteran astronaut John Young, who often narrated incidents about journey to the space, the moon and space shuttle. In her Test Pilot School classes, John Young would often discuss his space journeys to the Jet pilots sitting in the front row and Sunita with her few helicopter pilot friends sitting in the back row would listen to his accounts very carefully. Once he narrated how he learned to fly a helicopter in order to operate and the Lunar Lander, Sunita came to realise that she could also become an astronaut as the helicopter pilot also has a lot to do for the journey to the moon. From then, her thoughts encircled around the thought that she can also become an astronaut. Sunita also worked as the Squadron Safety officer and flew test flights in the SH-60B/F, UH1, AH-1W, Sh-2, VH-3, H-46, Ch53 and the H57.

Now Sunita was keen to be an astronaut. She researched on how it could be possible and applied for her Master's degree. She was deployed on board the USS Saipan when she was selected for the astronaut programme. She logged more than 2000 flight hours in about 3o aircrafts.

Path to be an Astronaut

Williams completed an M.S. in engineering management from the Florida Institute of Technology in Melbourne in 1995, and she entered astronaut training in 1998. She travelled to Moscow, where she received training in robotics and other International Space Station (ISS) operational technologies while working with the Russian Federal Space Agency and with crews preparing for expeditions to the ISS. After attaining her master's Degree she applied for the astronaut programme twice. She applied, and then finished her two years of test pilot school. "I had to go back to sea. It's called a disassociated sea tour. I would not be flying but still going back to sea. This is a way to get to appreciate the Navy." She landed an interview at the Johnson Space Centre, and then went back out on the ship.

> Sunita ended in a complete new world with a new beginning—she became an astronaut and achieved the impossible. In 1998, she was selected by the NASA and had her first flight in 2006. Since then, she has been up to the ISS four times—being the commander during her last trip in 2012.

"Six months later, there was one phone in our department. One rotary phone. I was living on the ship and everyone had left when the phone rang. Are you interested in coming to Johnson Space Centre to work in the astronaut programme. It was seven at night in the office. I had a celebration by myself," said Williams.

She started the program in August 1998. Later, after a period of training and evaluation she travelled to Moscow to work with the Russian Space Agency on their contribution to the International Space Station (ISS). In 2002, she spent nine days underwater in the Aquarius habitat off the coast of Florida as part of the NEEMO2 exploration mission.

Sunita recounts "Enjoy what you are doing, you'll naturally do well at it, and if [the opportunity to be an astronaut] comes up, it's just a bonus."

And to her greatest astonishment her wings spread—flying copters and then to the to the wide world of space. Sunita ended in a complete new world with a new beginning–she became an astronaut and achieved the impossible. In 1998, she was selected by the NASA and had her first flight in 2006. Since then, she has been up to the ISS four times—being the commander during her last trip in 2012. On Dec. 9, 2006, Williams launched into space for the first time on board the shuttle Discovery as part of the 14th expedition to the ISS. She remained in space till April 26, 2007. While there, she set a world record for females over the course of four space walks, spending 29 hours and 17 minutes outside of the station. (The record is now held by Peggy Whitson, who has spent almost 40 hours outside a vehicle over the course of six space walks.) Over the course of her 195 days in space, Williams also set a new record for females.

Williams is the second woman of Indian descent to go into space. Before Sunita, Kalpana Chawla made two shuttle flights, the first aboard Columbia in 1997 and in second time also abroad Columbia. But unfortunately the shuttle broke up during re-entry on February 1, 2003 and astraonaut Kalpana Chawla had to pay with her life.

The Dream-Come True – at NASA

"I can fly a Helicopter. May be I can go to space", that's what she thought while listening to the illustrious stories of space from John Young, the ninth astronaut to land on the moon. While her stay at the Test pilot school she listened with great attention to the stories of space journeys narrated by the astronaut. John Young had been on six space flights and had been a part of the team to the moon twice. Once he even drove a lunar vehicle on its surface. One fact that strongly remained in her mind was that the astronaut had to learn to fly the helicopter to prepare for moon landing. His experiences inspired her.

Right from her childhood she was very interested in knowing about space. When she was five years old she saw Neil Armstrong walking on the moon and thought like every child how if she could become an astronaut one day. She would watch TV shows about space travel with great interest.

Right from her childhood she was very interested in knowing about space. When she was five years old she saw Neil Armstrong walking on the moon and thought like every child how if she could become an astronaut one day. She would watch TV shows about space travel with great interest.

Mother Bonnie recounts, "President Kennedy had a great push for space travel. We watched this on TV and the first man was on the moon and the interesting things that were happening at that time – she was very true in tune to all that. It was probably something that she had at the back of her mind."

Perhaps Young's narrations boosted her dormant desire to become an astronaut. The seeds were latent in her mind and all that was needed a boost to her desires. There were so many pilots but only few astronauts. Sunita wanted to try her luck. But her dream seemed impossible. She started preparing herself to be one. Incidentally the USNA is credited with sending the highest number of students to the astronaut programme. Their number was so large that they celebrated Astronaut Convocation day and invited the Alumni to speak about their space sojourn. Also the top ranking students of the Naval Test pilot school opted for the astronaut programme. So, Sunita's road was not an unexplored one but she had her predecessors to follow.

Williams completed an M.S. in engineering management from the Florida Institute of Technology in Melbourne in 1995. After attaining her Master's Degree she applied for the astronaut programme twice. Later, after a period of training and evaluation she travelled to Moscow to work with the Russian Space Agency on their contribution to the International Space Station (ISS).

She applied at NASA but got rejected. As evident it was not easy to get into NASA so easily. Sunita did not give up. She prepared herself with great sincerity. She tried to acquire required qualifications. Williams completed an M.S. in engineering management from the Florida Institute of Technology in Melbourne in 1995. After attaining her Master's Degree she applied for the astronaut programme twice. Later, after a period of training and evaluation she travelled to Moscow to work with the Russian Space Agency on their contribution to the International Space Station (ISS).

She returned to the Test Pilot school and worked as an instructor and added strong points to her curriculum vitae. She reapplied at NASA and this time she was not disappointed. Sunita was one among the few lucky people who found her applications going through for the second time in a prestigious place like NASA.

It was in the summer of 1998, while she was in the ship USS Saipan at Norfolk, Virginia, she got an interview call from the astronaut office at Houston. She was overjoyed as she was nearing her destination. She got selection as an astronaut-in training. She entered astronaut training in 1998. Her journey began and at the same year she was selected to work on the space station project. She travelled to Moscow, where she received training in robotics and other International Space Station (ISS) operational technologies while working with the Russian Federal Space Agency and with crews preparing for expeditions to the ISS.

> Life at NASA was of about tough work and study of technical and engineering details. Before they could be actually called an astronaut they have to undergo a rigorous training of more than two years. The initial trainings included swimming tests, physical tasks for endurance and a list of other survival techniques.

"When you get here, training to fly is always a couple of years," she said. "After that, it's sort of like a waiting game.... The reality of actually going into space, people Don't actually think it is going to happen till you are sitting on that rocket and those engines fire." Her first flight was in 2006.

Near the end of November 2002, while waiting, she attended the national outdoor leadership school in the underwater habitat near Key Largo. Again, it was back to the ocean. She had an opportunity to go to Antarctica and collect meteorites. About a week before she was to leave for Antarctica, she was asked; Do you want to go to the International Space Station? "They were building the space station," said Williams. "There were all sorts of space walks going on at the time.

Life at NASA was of about tough work and study of technical and engineering details. Before they could be actually called an astronaut they have to undergo a rigorous training of more than two years. The initial trainings included swimming tests, physical tasks for endurance and a list of other survival techniques. At the beginning the astronauts in training undergoes orientation briefings along with technical and scientific briefings. Orientation of space station emphasised the aspects of energy control, emphasis on heating systems, power and motion control. Thereafter intensive sessions in Shuttle International Space Station Systems followed by psychological training and ground training follows. Sunita eagerly learned and prepared herself for the mission. She learned about her role in space odyssey and she updated herself with the knowledge of the culture, customs and their language.

Often, walking in space is considered a similar activity as that of walking in water. She swam 25 metre pool wearing a flight suit and swimming shoes. It was challenging.

The Space is actually a big void which is very different from that of the earth. Teaching survival technique in the space is actually more challenging because you cannot anticipate situations unlike ground-based missions. So how could someone prepare for the vast unknown? Here how the experience of previous space travellers and the ability of the human mind to anticipate things help them to come up with strategic planning and module that gives a fair idea of what to be taught. That is why astronauts in training had to undergo severe training schedules. Sunita underwent T-38 flight training, water and wilderness survival techniques etc.

Training was becoming tough every day. They had classroom sessions as well as sessions in stimulators, which actually taught them how it is to be within a version of actual space station. They are familiarised with the actual microgravity environment. The astronauts in training are enabled with skills of repairing, maintenance etc. They were extensively trained on all the activities they would do in the space.

When Sunita entered NASA, it was already five years when the plans for ISS was formulated. The two major countries Russia and USA are already at a high pace in building the modules required for building ISS. ISS was a huge project and it would take several years for completion. Like the earlier Mir the ISS is proposed to be a modular space station and it was evident that it would take a long time because the project was a huge one. Sunita and her fellow astronauts were trained and acquainted with both sides—the Russian and the American side. It was a combined effort of both the countries. Finally the modules were ready and and the first module to be used for launch of the ISS—the rocket Proton was ready. It was to carry the Russian module

When Sunita entered NASA, it was already five years when the plans for ISS was formulated. The two major countries Russia and USA are already at a high pace in building the modules required for building ISS. ISS was a huge project and it would take several years for completion.

Zyara on November 20, 1998 from Baikonur. Oncle Zarya was placed in the orbit, NASA prepared for the launch of its module Unity. Unity was launched by SS Endeavour—one of the five space shuttles that belonged to NASA.

Along with Unity Endeavour carried two astronauts Jerry Ross and James Newman. The two astronauts undertook the first extra vehicular activity (EVA) from the ISS and connected Zarya and Unity.

Robotics, Russians and Space

Sunita was privileged to be a part of NASA where she had seen history taking place in front of her eyes. After experiencing all these, she concentrated on her training with more vigour and dedication. She was already excited and was desperately waiting for her turn. Now her training sessions included interaction with those who have already undertaken the mission. She diligently concentrated on robotics, space walks and Russian language and also familiarised herself with the Russian language.

Since Robotics forms an integral part of the space travel and stay, Sunita underwent intensive training in the Robotics branch of the ISS, i.e., Special

Since Robotics forms an integral part of the space travel and stay, Sunita underwent intensive training in the Robotics branch of the ISS, i.e., Special Purpose Dexterous Manipulation. Robotics helped them to adjust in situations where there is an array of sophisticated instrumentation with restricted movement and no involvement of human interaction.

Purpose Dexterous Manipulation. Robotics helped them to adjust in situations where there is an array of sophisticated instrumentation with restricted movement and no involvement of human interaction.

Like every other specialised studies, the astronauts underwent special training in simulated situations that would be prevalent aboard space stations. The experience of the astronauts in this created simulated situations are recorded, recreated and practised in to perfection. The astronauts were prepared to face dire consequences while their stay in the space

Life in space is not easy. Unlike life on earth the life at zero gravity restricts your emotional expressions. You cannot crib over the phone with your friend or throw off things when you are angry. Team building was a very important thing every astronaut has to learn. In a close team the astronauts in a particular mission has to work for a long time irrespective of their personal likings or disliking. Sunita also underwent some mission specific training. They were given enough time to know their fellow astronauts. At longer space missions it so happens that the crewmen are confined to certain specific activities. There is no shopping, no dining out and nothing of that sort like spending lot of time talking to friends or wasting time gossiping. The small team worked together and there is actually no room for Claustrophobia. The astronauts therefore undergo NASA Extreme environment Mission Operations or NEEMO. Here the astronauts are sent underwater to the Aquarius, an undersea research station—the only one of its kind in the world. Training in the NEEMO helped the astronauts to adjust in space. The hostile, alien and tough atmosphere is not congenial for the astronauts. By adjusting to the situations at Aquarius the astronauts are exposed to a realistic atmosphere that is expected in space. Apart from that, they are exposed to microgravity situations everyday in order to make themselves adjustable to the atmosphere at space. During her training she continued to log into her flying hours and regularly practiced swimming her passion. The days were busy and she slowly headed towards realising her dream. She eagerly waited for that moment when she would be in the space shuttle.

❑

Footprints on Space

Challenging convention and pushing the frontiers of science, Williams has achieved a feat that not many women, or men, have and when you ask her if she would have done anything differently she says, "I just wish I was 20 years younger and get to do it again."

Till March 2016, Sunita Williams has undertaken seven space walks for about 50 hours and 40 minutes. She holds the seventh position among the list of most experienced space walkers. However she holds the records for total spacewalks by a woman.

By the time Sunita started her astronaut training there were several developments taking place in the field of space research. The United Nations underwent financial crisis to complete the design and development of the proposed space Station, Freedom. In 1993, the politicians of the country questioned the necessity of spending billions on constructing Freedo. During this period, Bill Clinton was the President of USA He came up with some innovative ideas to enable space research. The president decided to abandon the working on his own space station, instead he joined hands with the other countries and worked together to build a space station. Russia was in a progressing state. It was building the space station Mir 2 and the Europeans were setting up Columbus (in the name of Christopher Columbus the sailor). The Japanese were also not far behind. They were building Kibo. The president of America came to terms to work together towards conquering the space. Perhaps this was the most remarkable decision of the twentieth Century to bring about international unity. USA together with Russia paced up to construct the International Space Station bridging the gap between them.

It was a huge project and both Russia and the US was busy constructing its modules. It was supposed to be a modular space station like Mir 2 built by Russia. Delay was evident because it took really long time to construct the modules. Finally on 20 November 1998, the first module that would initiate the starting of the ISS was ready for launch.

The ISS remained an idea alone till five years of Sunita's stay at NASA. It was a huge project and both Russia and the US was busy constructing its modules. It was supposed to be a modular space station like Mir 2 built by Russia. Delay was evident because it took really long time to construct the modules. Finally on 20 November 1998, the first module that would initiate the starting of the ISS was ready for launch. It was built by Russia and was named Zarya and the rocket Proton would carry it to be launched from Baikonur. Once Zarya was launched the next module by NASA, Unity was made ready by the scientists. It was launched by the SS Endeavour—one of the first shuttles that NASA had ownership. The Shuttle carried two astronauts also—James Newman and Jerry Ross. They connected Unity with Zarya and set out the first ever EVA on ISS.

> During her training Sunita learned Russian and went to Yuri Gagarin Cosmonaut Training Centre, located in Star City, Moscow. Sunita speaks Russian fluently and her stay at the training centre left a far-reaching impact on her. When she adopted her pet the Jack Russek Terrier, she named him Gorby after the name of the Russian president Mikhial Gorbachev.

Meanwhile, Sunita had almost done with her astronaut training. Fueled by her strong determination and undeterred spirit, Williams completed NASA's two-and-a-half year long astronaut training, which included intensive instruction in spacecraft and ISS systems, physiological and T-38 flight training, extravehicular activities (EVAs), robotic operations, as well as preparing for emergencies. "There are a lot of things that need to go right and there are many things that can go wrong, so we spend a lot of time learning how to deal with those emergencies," she says. "And then of course, the modules themselves—the European module Columbus, the Japanese module Gem, the U.S laboratory, the Canadian arm, and the Russian side of the space station. We need to know how to operate all those."

The mission to the ISS continued and the Russian Zvexda was launched in the year 2000. By now the ISS could man at least two men in it and it has become inhabitable. The space mission paced up. The modules were send one after another to construct the ISS. Work was in a good pace leading Sunita much nearer to her dream.

As a result hot air entered the wing when it re entered the earth's atmosphere and disintegrated SS Colombus killing all seven astronauts on board. This incident was one of the biggest tragedies in the space history of space missions. Sunita was very upset. She broke down and was devastated. She was in Hawaii when the tragedy occurred and cried in agony.

During her training Sunita learned Russian and went to Yuri Gagarin Cosmonaut Training Centre, located in Star City, Moscow. Sunita speaks Russian fluently and her stay at the training centre left a far-reaching impact on her. When she adopted her pet the Jack Russek Terrier, she named him Gorby after the name of the Russian president Mikhial Gorbachev. The Star city was once popular as the Closed Military Townlet during the Cold War days. It is a home for several cosmonaut and their families. The training centre is more than a century old where cosmonauts all over the world came for training. Though most of the training astronauts are Russians from Soviet Union there are people coming from all over the world. NASA sends its first astronaut batch in the year 1973. Their presence became more prominent when two astronauts came to train themselves for the Mir mission in the year

1994. Nowadays you will find astronauts spending long durations in Star City.

Sunita's astronaut training progressed steadily. She was expecting her first mission in a five years time. To her surprise one day in the winter of 2002, Charlie Precourt, the chief of the Astronaut office informed her that she has been selected for a space mission. She could not believe what she heard. She was very excited to know that her dream was slowly turning to reality. There was already another astronaut of Indian origin, Kalpana Chawla who was to undertake the space mission as a mission specialist at SS Columbia. The SS Columbia was scheduled to launch on 16 January 2003. The crew members included Michael Anderson, Laurel Clark, William McCool Ilan Ramon and Kalpana Chawla. SS Columbia was supposed to stay in space for sixteen days. However after completion of the mission while it re-entered as per the schedule, the shuttle caught fire and disintegrated. The cause of the disintegration was later assumed to be due to damage of thermal protection system. While landing, as it entered the earth's atmosphere the shuttle's foam insulation that protested it from heat fell off on to the left wing. As a result hot air entered the wing when it re entered the earth's atmosphere and disintegrated SS Colombus killing all seven astronauts on board. This incident was one of the biggest tragedies in the space history of space missions. Sunita was very upset. She broke down and was devastated. She was in Hawaii when the tragedy occurred and cried in agony. She said, "The overwhelming emotion was disbelief. Secondly, we just lost seven friends."

The Columbia tragedy was a tremendous learning experience for the scientists at NASA. The concept of the Space missions now took a different turn and all the remaining space shuttles of NASA were grounded. Extensive analysis was made to avoid untoward happening that might occur in the upcoming missions. The construction of ISS was put on hold and the missions were postponed delaying Sunita's proposed space travel. The tragedy shattered them. The astronauts-in training, the 1998 batch described themselves as Penguins- the birds that are unable to fly. Sunita was also a trainee of this batch. Sunita, who was a passionate blogger expressed their situation by saying, "Patience is a virtue, I think all of us have".

> Construction of the ISS essentially stopped until the space shuttle started flying again. Only after 2005 the operations resumed with the proposed launch of the shuttle SS Discovery. Sunita was now all set to go for a space mission in 2006. Her long awaited dream was about to come true. It was already eight years since she entered NASA.

And they did figure it out. "I'm pretty amazed by the talent and ability to pinpoint exactly what happened," said Williams. On liftoff, said Williams, foam on the external tank fell off and hit the left wing, and made a hole in the wing. This hole caused the catastrophe on re-entry into the atmosphere. NASA learned from what happened, made adjustments, and the mission continued. But for two years NASA suspended all space shuttle flights to the ISS, which had been under construction since 1998.

It took many years to return to normal work at NASA. Only the smaller Russian Soyuz spacecraft was going there.

Unlike the space shuttle, which carried seven people, the Soyuz only carried three. "Everybody had their doubts at first whether we were really going to go back," said Williams. But NASA found the cause and life went on, and they really were going back. Construction of the ISS essentially stopped until the space shuttle started flying again.

Only after 2005 the operations resumed with the proposed launch of the shuttle SS Discovery. Sunita was now all set to go for a space mission in 2006. Her long awaited dream was about to come true. It was already eight years since she entered NASA.

On December 9, 2006, Sunita's parents, Deepak and Bonnie Pandya along with friends, well-wishers and other near and dear ones came to Cape Canaveral, Florida to witness the historic moment of the launching of Shuttle Discovery. The Zalokars from Ohio and other parts of America and the Pandya's far from India waited with their fingers crossed to see Sunita flying space.

"Our flight was the third flight after we started flying again after the accident." She understood the risk, and noted the challenge NASA has always faced. "It's space," said Williams. "It is pretty dynamic and fast. How do you plan for something you have no idea what to plan for?" She said, of earth compared to space, "It's a 2-D world down here. If something bad happens in your car, you can pull over."

And as the launch date approached, it was again like a military deployment, as she "squared things away with my family." In case something bad happens, she said, NASA has a plan in place, as Williams noted for the Columbia disaster, for someone to work with the families. "You pick someone that your spouse will get along with," she said. She "spent a week in Massachusetts" visiting her family, she said. "I think they were fairly psyched till we got to Florida. And then the situation began to get nerve-wracking for them."

Astronauts have a training plan that marks progress as they prepare for launch. As they check things off on the training plan - x number of simulations etc. - they know they are getting closer to being ready, she said. And beyond the physical and mental skills required, Williams noted the crew is carefully created. Beyond bringing people of varying skills - spacewalking, robotic arms, etc.—to the space station, Williams said that a crew working in tight quarters obviously has to get along.

On December 9, 2006, Sunita's parents, Deepak and Bonnie Pandya along with friends, well-wishers and other near and dear ones came to Cape Canaveral, Florida to witness the historic moment of the launching of Shuttle Discovery. The Zalokars from Ohio and other parts of America and the Pandya's far from India waited with their fingers crossed to see Sunita flying space. The eagerly awaited with their eyes fixed to have a glimpse of their daughter. However, the astronauts were in quarantine for the last one week. They were in quarantine in order to prevent themselves from catching any sort of infections from the visitors. To fall sick during the mission in the ISS would actually create great inconvenience and problem. At last the moment came. Deepak Pandya recalls, we saw her just before the lift off but this time they were already in quarantine and we had to maintain a distance.

She talked to us and said 'Namaste' to everyone." With rituals and tradition the trip started. A Hindu priest recited a mantra for safety during the mission however the launch was postponed due to the clouds. Reminiscing the historic moment Deepak Pandya says, "When we saw her next she was already in the space shuttle right on top. We were awestruck and kept watching. The countdown started, there was a huge glow. We were too excited but at the same time apprehensive too. All of us remained silent and remained praying. Then suddenly with a thundering sound the shuttle blasted and within a few seconds the mission began. Later on when we saw a video of Sunita during the launch she was happy."

❑

Reflections of the Launch.....

With 24 hours to go—L-24 hours—"you're life becomes part of this L- time frame," said Williams. Things are going on. The count starts, the clock is ticking... everything is choreographed." The launch was at 11 pm. 'Our wake up time was noon," she said. "It was college hours, which was comforting.'

She had to test out her suit, getting in it with the help of a "suit technician" and then there is a pressure checks to be sure the suit holds pressure. Her husband, brother, sister and parents were in town and they had dinner together, then after the protective structure around the Space Shuttle was removed, the family took a ride out to see it. "It was really spectacular," she said.

All the time, the clock is "ticking, ticking, ticking closer," said Williams. There are personal details to be taken care of, she said. "You figure out if your digestive system is working correctly... You go to the bathroom one final time. Once in you are in your suit, you are wearing a diaper." As the astronauts are driven out the launch pad, Williams said, "It's just sort of surreal. Wow, this is really going to happen. I'd been out to the launch pad before. But the spacecraft wasn't filled with fuel." And seeing it like that, she said, "it seems like it's alive. It's plugged into a giant umbilical cord, getting data from the control centre." It was night time. It was raining. There is an elevator, a 195-foot tunnel, and then a white room where the astronauts put on parachutes. And then they climbed into the spacecraft. "There is a process to close the hatch. Do a pressure check. This time frame allows for anyone who has an issue with their suit to deal with it," she said. She spoke of "the whole process of the computer taking over. It's a pretty detailed process. We really aren't that involved till the very end."

There is an elevator, a 195-foot tunnel, and then a white room where the astronauts put on parachutes. And then they climbed into the spacecraft. "There is a process to close the hatch. Do a pressure check.

"There are fairly complicated commands that are being sent. We are there to answer the phone." There is more of course. "Inside the shuttle there are lots of switches. All of those switches should already be in configuration." If something needs adjusting, an astronaut is there to adjust it."

That was not Williams' role. "I was essentially cargo they were dropping off at the space station," she said. She was on the main deck. "The two other men on the main deck were also rookies." They held their hands up in the air, a sort of thumbs up. "All three of us were screaming like we were on a roller coaster," said Williams. The first 30 seconds of acceleration, she could feel the G-forces crushing her. It was hard to breathe. She was warned of it. "At first you are like, oh, that's what they were talking about. And then, it's going to be over. It's going to be over. It's going to be all right." After the first minute and a half, she said, "the atmosphere is becoming thinner and we are going faster and faster."

"Forty-eight hours makes a tremendous difference," NASA launch director Mike Leinbach told Discovery's crew shortly before the launch. "The weather is outstanding, the vehicle's in great shape, so we wish you all good luck, Godspeed and we'll see you back here in 12 days."

In 7-1/2 minutes, they were in orbit, she said. "Everything becomes slow and floaty... Finally we're here. Then you realize what floating is. You take your gloves off and they float. It's funny, but weird."

Of course it was a time to rejoice. It was a dream-come-true after. After dedication of eight years, On December 9, 2006, Sunita Williams was launched to the International Space Station (ISS) with STS-116, aboard the Space Shuttle Discovery. She was sent to join the Expedition 14 crew.

Space was the Destiny

So the journey began crossing the limits and reaching the unknown. Sunita Williams and her crew members are now heading towards another world—unpredictable and unique.

In addition to Williams and Polansky, the crew includes Sweden's first astronaut, Christer Fuglesang, pilot William Oefelein, flight engineer Robert Curbeam, and mission specialists Nicholas Patrick, and Joan Higginbotham.

> Williams' mission, the 20th to the space station, will include a complex set of tasks carried out over three spacewalks, including adding a small structural truss to the orbiting laboratory and reconfiguring the station's electrical system to begin drawing power from solar panels added on the last mission.

"Forty-eight hours makes a tremendous difference," NASA launch director Mike Leinbach told Discovery's crew shortly before the launch. "The weather is outstanding, the vehicle's in great shape, so we wish you all good luck, Godspeed and we'll see you back here in 12 days."

"We look forward to lighting up the night sky." That is what Discovery commander Mark Polansky replied when they were about to begin the journey to the space.

About her entry in the shuttle, Sunita says, "The space shuttle is exactly that, a shuttle. They dropped me off and took another guy back home." "When you see that shuttle leave and fly away," said Williams, "you're stomach drops. Oh dear, they're going to earth. I'm here." Again, she compared it to being on deployment. The feeling "was familiar to me, a Navy guy."

Still, she said, it was emotional. "I'll be honest. I cried a bit. And then I went up and had dinner with the guys." Her attitude after that brief moment of reflection was, "Get to work, you chucklehead."

Now the crew was all set to be in space for a 12-day mission where they will rewire the space station's electrical system, a crucial step in NASA's plan to finish building the outpost before the shuttles stop flying in four years. Williams' mission, the 20th to the space station, will include a complex set of tasks carried out over three spacewalks, including adding a small structural truss to the orbiting laboratory and reconfiguring the station's electrical system to begin drawing power from solar panels added on the last mission.

> Sunita was a part of the Expedition 14 team wzzhere Michael Lopex Alegria or LA (His crewman referred to him often) was its other crewmate was Mikhailtyurin or Misha. These two astronauts arrived at the ISS on September 20, 2006, long before Sunita came here. They were launched here on a Soyuz from Baikonur.

The launch of Discovery was the third space shuttle mission in six months. The astronauts will also move an older set of solar arrays out of the way of the new arrays, which will turn on their axis like a paddle wheel as the station follows its orbital path. The mission planned to replace German astronaut Thomas Reiter with Williams who resided in the space station for five and a half months in residence along with two other astronauts.

After the Columbia disaster, night launches were banned. The fuel tank was redesigned to ensure untoward happening. Discovery is scheduled to land December 21 at the Kennedy Space Centre. It will bring back to earth German Thomas Reiter of the European Space Agency in place of Williams who will spend six months at the

International Space station along with a Russian and an American astronaut. Sunita along with Mark Polansky (Commander), Mission specialist Joan Higginbotham, Nicholas Patrick, Christer Fuglesang, Robert Curbeam and pilot William Oefelein, all of them were carried in the space shuttle Discovery which can carry seven astronauts at a time. However all these astronauts were not on a long term mission like Sunita. They were supposed to return to earth before Christmas after completion of their 12 day mission to work on constructions of the ISS. Sunita was a part of the Expedition 14 team wzzhere Michael Lopex Alegria or LA (His crewman referred to him often) was its other crewmate was Mikhailtyurin or Misha. These two astronauts arrived at the ISS on September 20, 2006, long before Sunita came here. They were launched here on a Soyuz from Baikonur.

The ISS revolves that point twice day for ten minutes and the launch has to take place within that short span of time. Once it does the shuttle orbit around earth. However the average time to dock at the ISS is of two days during the time Sunita went to space. After March 2013, the docking time is reduced to six hours making the same day launch and docking easier.

Finally on December 11, 2006, the Discovery with six other crew took off at 8:47:35 pm. Saturday (7:17: 35 am IST Sunday) on a column of fire that briefly dispelled the darkness over the Kennedy Space Centre at Cape Canaveral, Florida. With the successful launch, Discovery crew member Christer Fugelsang of Sweden becomes the first Scandinavian in space.

About this glorious moments Sunita vividly describes in her

blog which she maintains regularly even during her stay at the space. In her post about the launch she wrote, ‘Getting into space is quite a jolt! Needless to say, besides the brain, the rest of the body takes time to adjust. The first six hours of being in-orbit were a little difficult. I think things just didn’t know where to go.... The auxiliary power units start up, the vehicle begins vibrating and we are rumbling and shaking pretty significantly. Now it seemed like we were really, really going to go. Then the blast of the solid rockek boosters launched us right off the pad. I don’t think my stomach knew what was going at all!’

As the shuttle paced up Sunita recounts, “we started to accelerate like nobody’s business... our stomachs and the rest of us are really getting squished now-....we were still accelerating through the thinning of atmosphere. Then everything got quiet. My pet started to float and my arms started to float too. We were hooting and shouting the entire time...Joanie, Christer and I were all there shaking hands and shouting for the entire ride, a sort of like screaming on roller coaster. When we were there, we could not stop laughing”.

The shuttle takes almost eight minutes to launch. Once it reaches the earth’s orbit it circles the Earth before docking. The ISS is also not stationary. It has to dock in the ISS which is cruising a t a speed of 17,500 miles per hour. That means the ISS orbits round the earth at a speed of seven kilometres per second. So it was not an easy task for a shuttle to dock in the ever moving ISS that too at such a speed in the space. Moreover among so many objects floating around it was a difficult task to locate the ISS and dock there and land its crew. It was actually a difficult task. The Launch Control team monitored the launch of the shuttle and planned out the launch time and the lift off in such a way that by the time the shuttle reaches space it is ahead of the ISS orbiting over that point. The ISS revolves that point twice day for ten minutes and the launch has to take place within that short span of time. Once it does the shuttle orbit around earth. However the average time to dock at the ISS is of two days during the time Sunita went to space. After March 2013, the docking time is reduced to six hours making the same day launch and docking easier.

By the time the shuttle docks, the crew establishes connection with the station and prepare to enter the ISS. Sunita was aware that she should know floating in order to launch. She practised by banging in to the corners along with her team. They all prepared themselves for their stay in space.... wearing space suits, getting out of it and then rolling in and out of sleeping bags...all formed a part of their preparations. So regular packing and unpacking followed.... Mark Polansky gave Sunita the astronauts wing another tradition to be followed in space. Sunita took some days to adapt to the situation but she did it. Later on she commented, "We have amazing bodies which just automatically can adapt to the surroundings. Never take your body for granted—keep it healthy."

The astronauts have adapted themselves to the surroundings. Now, the control of the mission after the launch is taken over by the Mission Control Centre, popularly known by its radio call sign 'Houston'—the Christopher C, Kraft Jr Mission Control Centre. It is from her the entire mission is managed and monitored. It is functional 24x7 because there are one or the other astronauts working in the ISS every day. It is a busy place with engineers, robotics specialists, flight controllers all controlling and monitoring their respective activities. The astronauts on board are in constant communication with the Mission Control Centre.

❑

Know the ISS

The men in it.....

The International Space Station is a Joint venture undertaken primarily by five space agencies, including National Aeronautics and Space Agency, Russian Federal Space agency, Japan Aero Space Exploration Agency, Canadian Space Agency and the European Space Agency. Apart from that the Brazilian Space Agency and the Italian Space Agency works in separate contract with NASA where the Italian Space Agency operates outside the framework of ESA. The legality of the ISS was decided through an International treaty where fifteen governments participated. The treaty was signed on 28 January 1998 and the countries that participated include Canada, The US, Japan, Russian Federation and eleven members of ESA.

> The ISS is somewhat like a ship. Therefore several terms used in the ship are used to describe different places in the ISS. The left and the right sides of the ISS are called the Port and the Starboard and so many other nautical terms. The rear and the front are called Forward and Aft, the top as the overhead and the bottom as Deck.

It was a team effort to build the ISS. The Progress Spacecrafts carried the logistics required for the constructions and also the food for the astronauts. There were forty assembly flights and about thirty utilisation flights were involved throughout the project. The experimental equipment, fuel and consumables were supplied to the space station through the European ATV (Automated Transfer Vehicle), the Japanese HTV (H II Transfer Vehicle). Now the Space station after its completion has a pressurised volume of 1,000 cubic metres, a mass of 400,000 kilograms, 100 kilowatts of power output, and 108.4 metres long truss, 74 metres long modules and it can accommodate around six members.

It is located in an orbit round the earth at an approximate altitude of 360 km and it travels at an average speed of 27,744 km/hour, completing 15.7 orbits around the earth a day. From the time of its launch on November 20, 1998 till the time Sunita landed on it the ISS completed over 46,000 orbits round the earth.

Have you imagined how the different places in the ISS are described as? It is quite interesting. The ISS is somewhat like a ship. Therefore several terms used in the ship are used to describe different places in the ISS. The left and the right sides of the ISS are called the Port and the Starboard and so many other nautical terms. The rear and the front are called Forward and Aft, the top as the overhead and the bottom as Deck. The connection of Navy and Space is somehow inseparable. The first commander of the ISS was a Navy officer who introduced several naval traditions in the Space ship also. The first commander, Bill Shepherd not only coined the radio sign 'Alpha', but also introduced the custom of ringing the bell. The bell that hung in the ISS was ringed by the new and visiting crewmen announcing their arrival in ISS. Moreover after introducing the term Alpha, the astronauts from ISS call the mission control team by saying "Houston, this is Alpha calling..." Later on the phrase became a frequent term among the astronauts calling the Mission Control team.

The person who heads the mission is termed as the Commander. He is a man of experience usually having experience in several voyages or expedition. There is another person who is a mission specialist assigned with various specific duties while aboard the ISS.

All the space shuttles are named after ships, she said, so it is only fitting that the new research ship would be named after an astronaut. And having spent two extended tours about the International Space Station (ISS), Williams drew the parallel between space and sea exploration.

Another interesting fact about the ISS is that the crew in the space station has been ranked with particular designations. The person who heads the mission is termed as the Commander. He is a man of experience usually having experience in several voyages or expedition. There is another person who is a mission specialist assigned with various specific duties while aboard the ISS.

> It had the Russian module Zarya which means Sunrise, the US module destiny and the two modules connected by Unity. It has an Airlock called the Quest, a docking area known as the Piers. Another important segment of the ISS is Zvezda which means the star is the living segment of the station.

Another most important designation in the ISS is the Pilot who usually assists the Commander, so he is supposed to have a similar experience as the commander. Only difference is that the pilot need not have prior space experience.

Flight Engineer assists the commander and the pilot the same way as the mission specialist does but he should be a competent pilot too. The scientific officer on board is generally a scientist that performs the experiments that is usually carried in the ISS. Imagine there is also another participant astronaut who can enjoy a space travel—an impossible dream for many of us. He is the Space flight participant—who is a tourist to the ISS. He is not assigned with any duties but a luxury traveller that enjoys space travel like any other tourists

The construction of the ISS continued till 2010 and it was almost a different ISS when Sunita landed in the year 2012. By 2010 it became a fully functioning laboratory orbiting around the earth. ISS was huge now like a football field with giant solar panels forming its wings weighing over 4,00,000 kgs and it had the Russia, US, Japanese and European modules. I can now carry six astronauts.

The ISS derives its energy from the sun whose light is converted to electricity through the use of solar arrays attached to its permanent truss structure. The atmospheric pressure, oxygen levels, water, fire and fire extinguishing etc. are controlled by the ISS Environmental Control and Life Support System. The atmosphere in the space station is given the highest priority by the support system but the system also collects process and stores and wastes used and produced by the crew. The use of activated charcoal is the primary method of removing the excreta of human metabolism from the air.

ISS.... Odyssey... the New Chapter

ISS was all set by the time Sunita arrived. It had the Russian module Zarya which means Sunrise, the US module destiny and the two modules connected by Unity. It has an Airlock called the Quest, a docking area known as the Piers. Another important segment of the ISS is Zvezda which means the star is the living segment of the station. This is the place where the astronauts gathered for their meals and after work rest.

Finally on December 11, 2006, Sunita arrived at the ISS. An amazing experience ... She woke up to the famous strains of the Beatles song "Here Comes the Sun". The work began. It was unlike duties on earth. Life paced up and she could take three holidays a week but had to adjust the holidays in such a way that it suited the needs of the multi ethnic crew. With serious activities, they had fun and lighter moments. Sunita tried her culinary skills learned from her mother. She made Sushi but in a zero gravity atmosphere the Wasabi got scattered in the space station. Sunita had a tough time cleaning. The spicy greenish condiment squirted out of a tube while Sunita tried to have it with her packaged

Salmon. It is a real mess. Sunita recollects the incident and tells her mother, "We cleaned up off the walls. We finally got the easabi smell out after it was flying around everywhere." The wasabi tube banished and reached a Cargo vehicle and stayed packed away. Later she recollects, "I don't think we are going to use it again. It is too dangerous."

Astronauts usually do not carry a lot of luggage. They can dispense with only a few clothes because nothing gets dirty there. They didn't have a laundry in the ISS to wash their clothes. The only way to get rid of their old clothes is that they wait for the new load of clothes to arrive. Food is sent in a preserved form. Like laundry there is no kitchen in the ISS too. The provisions hardly get exhausted because every few months vehicles called the Progress are sent to the ISS loaded with food, equipment, clothes and other necessary items for conducting experiments. These vehicles dock in the ISS till the next vehicle arrives. Later, the thrash is loaded in these vehicles and they are disconnected. Since after unlocking the vehicle loses its ability to remain in the orbit it is destroyed in space.

Food is sent in a preserved form. Like laundry there is no kitchen in the ISS too. The provisions hardly get exhausted because every few months vehicles called the Progress are sent to the ISS loaded with food, equipment, clothes and other necessary items for conducting experiments.

So, life without a kitchen! How could a foodie survive in such a situation! Each of the crew members are given quite a number of bonus packs of their favourite food which helps them to endure in space for a longer time.

The astronauts usually worked in their respective modules every day. Sunita was also assigned with a list of task for the day. The ISS did not have electricians, plumbers, maintenance workers, cleaners, mechanics, etc., to help them in everyday affairs. It was the duty of the crew to do all the maintenance work—be it mending the toilet flush or some problem in the mechanics—whatever comes their way. Besides carrying out experiments, construction work and any other work related to the space station Sunita was assigned with cleaning and maintenance work also. After all these tasks the crew eagerly waited for the meal time in the evenings. Sunita's containers often came out with certain spicy Indian cuisines as the palak paneer and the Punjabi chole, halwa, etc. They were also enabled with their favourite shows like the football and the favourite TV shows. They would eagerly wait for the weekends for their favourite shows.

Williams prepared for the space walks with great sincerity. Exercise formed an integral part of the preparation. It was a routine activity in the ISS and a daily regimen was essential to maintain bone and muscle in micro gravity.

Spacewalks....

There was a timeline to get on. "We had three spacewalks coming up for reconfiguring the heating and cooling system," said Williams.

Williams prepared for the space walks with great sincerity. Exercise formed an integral part of the preparation. It was a routine activity in the ISS and a daily regimen was essential to maintain bone and muscle in micro gravity. The routine activity was a mini triathlon comprising twenty-five minute biking, twenty minutes (2.7 km) running and several laps of floating, somewhat similar to that of swimming. The treadmill was engineered in such a way that when an astronaut exercise on it the whole space station should not vibrate. The treadmill is called the TVIS or the Treadmill Vibration Isolation System and the bike is known as the CEVIS, i.e., the Cycle Ergometer Vibration Isolation System and the weight lifting Device called the ARED which is the Advanced Resistive exercise Device. Also to keep the muscles they practised catching of different objects with the help of feet, grasped objects and lifted weight.

They were allowed to walk inside the space station. However on 16 December 2006 Sunita along with Bob Curbeam moved outside the confines of ISS and completed rewiring of the International Space Station. It took them almost 7 hours and 31 minutes.

The construction of the ISS progressed. Sunita had to prepare for EVA which required a great deal of preparation, including the charging of the space suit and reviewing of the tools. Everything is planned and rechecked again and again because the experiments and repairs are actually done outside the ISS. All equipments are checked and rechecked because once you are on an EVA you cannot just ask for an equipment from outside. A large part of the preparation of the space walk is often referred as the 'pre-breathe'. In this process the nitrogen in the body is removed by breathing in higher concentration of oxygen. This is done to avoid certain conditions while in the EVA away from the ISS atmosphere.

During their EVA, astronauts might suffer from severe joint, elbows, and knee and shoulder pains due to formation of air bubbles inside the body. These kinds of pains are known as 'the bends'. Often bends happen to the divers when they hit the surface of the water on their way up. In order to cope up these adversities, the astronauts wear their space suits, several hours before they leave the station. The suits are usually filled in with oxygen and the participant astronauts breathe in this pure oxygen thereby splashing out the nitrogen of the body.

> By now Sunita has broken the record of maximum spacewalks done by a woman. Sunita Williams remained outside the ISS for 6 hours and 40 minutes to complete three spacewalks in nine days. By logging 29 hours and 17 minutes in four spacewalks she eclipsed the record held by Kathryn C. Thornton for most spacewalk time by a woman.

The astronauts also wore a SAFER or simplified aid for EVA rescue. So whenever an astronaut tends to float or the tether comes loose the SAFER is used to pull back them to the Station. These are controlled a joystick. The most interesting fact about the EVA is that the astronaut works here continuously and they don't have loo breaks. Therefore to survive for such long hours the astronauts wear diapers.

They were allowed to walk inside the space station. However on 16 December 2006 Sunita along with Bob Curbeam moved outside the confines of ISS and completed rewiring of the International Space Station. It took them almost 7 hours and 31 minutes. When she did her first spacewalk, "Honestly, I was not scared at first. It was night time. Everything is very well choreographed and planned. I knew exactly what I was doing," she said. "And then the sun came up," she said. The ISS orbits the earth every 92 minutes.

"Oh God," she thought. "We are flying across the planet and I am sitting here outside in my suit." While in awe at the experience, "compartmentalization," allowed her to continue her work, she said. And then she crossed the sun, shining on the planet and on her and, she said, "you can actually see how fast you are going." Of course her job involved more than the spacewalks and the heating system.

Then onwards she completed other three space walks on 31st January and 4th and 9th February with Michael Lopez-Alegria, the third space walk lasting for 6hours and forty minutes. By now Sunita has broken the record of maximum spacewalks done by a woman. Sunita Williams remained outside the ISS for 6 hours and 40 minutes to complete three spacewalks in nine days. By logging 29 hours and 17 minutes in four spacewalks she eclipsed the record held by Kathryn C. Thornton for most spacewalk time by a woman.

During her fourth space walk on December 18, 2007 of Expedition 16, Williams was surpassed by Peggy Whitson with a cumulative EVA time of 32 hours, 36 minutes. While outside, Sunita had a view of Pantagonia of South America and the most amazing view of our planet. She wrote, "we really have the most beautiful planet in the solar system. None other has blue water and white clouds covering colourful landmasses filled with thriving, beautiful living beings like human beings… I do hope there are other wonderful planets living and thriving out there, but ours is special because it is ours and ours to take care of. We really can't take that too lightly."

"And then the sun came up," she said. The ISS orbits the earth every 92 minutes. "How amazing," she thought. "We are flying across the planet and I am sitting here outside in my suit."

On April 26, 2007, NASA decided to bring Williams back to Earth on the STS-117 mission aboard Atlantis. She did not break the US single spaceflight record that was recently broken by former crew member Commander Michael Lopez-Alegria, but did break the record for longest single spaceflight by a woman.

While in awe at the experience, "compartmentalization," allowed her to continue her work, she said. And then she crossed the sun, shining on the planet and on her and, she said, "you can actually see how fast you are going."

Sunita's spacewalks were a unique experience for her. About the spacewalks she tells, "I was amazed that you can look all around 36o degrees and see everything and to really see the whole horizon, the curvature of the earth and all the stars as well, was just spectacular, and while we were out then we had the opportunity to see the Aurora, the Northern Lights, and that was just a little bit creepy because it was this green shadow thing coming over the earth. It was pretty spectacular, and i think the others were also pretty amazed at that type of view.'

She was assigned to the International Space Station and she extended her service as a member of Expedition 14 and Expedition 15. In April 2007, the Russian members of the crew rotated, changing to Expedition 15.

On April 26, 2007, NASA decided to bring Williams back to Earth on the STS-117 mission aboard Atlantis. She did not break the US single spaceflight record that was recently broken by former crew member Commander Michael López-Alegría, but did break the record for longest single spaceflight by a woman.

Sunita felt that walking in space and looking outside refreshed her geography lessons. Nor did she forget the history and her origin. On January 11, 2007, Thursday she sent a message of congratulations to the Indian space scientists on the successful launch of PSLV.

Back to Earth....

"Exploration isn't necessary or logical. It is something that comes from inside each and every one of us. I believe we are all born with the curiosity for exploration. Human space flight is one aspect of it and it is one that I have been intimately familiar with for the past six months." It is beginning of the farewell speech of Sunita Williams after completion of her first mission in the ISS that echoes in the ISS.

It was time to move forward. The arrival of next set of the cosmonaut meant the end of the mission and the beginning of the next mission. On 9 April 2007 Cosmonauts Fyodor Yurchikhin and Oleg Ktov arrived on a Soyuz launch vehicle from Baikonur. It marked the end of Expedition 14 and the beginning of Expedition 15. Along with them came a space tourist named Charles Simyoni, a Hungarian-American who after two weeks later returned to earth on April 21 on Soyuz.

The SS Atlantis was originally scheduled to pick her up in April but she ended up staying at the space till June 22.

Initially her first space journey was supposed to be of six months. Because the flight that was supposed to carry her back home was hit by hail, her return to earth was delayed and she had to stay there for 195 days.

> She was happy because her dream came true but sad to leave the ISS. Her farewell speech saw her choking back tears, "I'm sad to say goodbye but it is time for the International Space station to grow a little more. You, the ISS will always be a part of me as you are a part of so many. You will pave the way for our future."

It was time to return home. Mixed feelings of happiness and sorrow filled Sunita's mind. She was happy because her dream came true but sad to leave the ISS. Her farewell speech saw her choking back tears, "I'm sad to say goodbye but it is time for the International Space station to grow a little more. You, the ISS will always be a part of me as you are a part of so many. You will pave the way for our future." In her tribute to the fellow astronauts, ground crew, technicians and the engineers, she said, "these folks, along with their families have dedicated their lives to ensure the success of astronauts and cosmonauts—along with exploration for the next generation".

"What people are worried about when you are in space a long time is that you are exposed to extensive radiation," she said. Leaving the ISS was sad, she said. "You feel a slight ownership of the space station. It's like one of your kids. It's sad to leave. Part of it is you don't know if you are ever going to get the opportunity to come back."

In her mind, she had scoffed at the idea that returning to Earth would be difficult. “My impression when I was up in space was I didn’t believe I wouldn’t feel good when I came home,” said Williams.

But the return home actually “hit me like a ton of bricks,” she said. “You can’t simulate gravity. “I threw up after I came home. People do,” said Williams. “Your balance system is off.” She explained. “There is fluid in your ears, under the influence of gravity. When you are in space, that stuff floats and your whole cognitive system changes. Your brain has to go, this is gravity.” “For me, it was like two days,” said Williams. Knowing others had already been through it helped, she said. Stimulating muscles by walking, and picking her knees up while walking, also helped.

It is a difficult task to adjust your body to the gravity as the body changes in zero gravity atmospheres.

“Small things like lifting up your head with your neck take work. Your head feels heavy. The muscles (supporting the head) haven’t had anything to do for six months.” “Eventually you get it back again,” said Williams. “Initially, it’s tough.”

After serving as a mission specialist, she returned to Earth on at the end of the STS-117 mission on June 22, 2007. Poor weather at the Kennedy Space Centre in Cape Canaveral forced mission managers to skip three landing attempts there over previous 24 hours. They then diverted Atlantis to Edwards Air Force Base in California, where the shuttle touched down at 3:49 pm EDT, returning Williams home after a record 192-day stay in space. She landed at the Edwards Air force Base in California. To receive her after the iconic journey her sister Dina waited there and did so her beloved pet Gorby. The Jack Terrier, without whom the story of Sunita Williams will be incomplete.

❑

The Mission STS-116

Preparation for its Journey

STS 116 was a Space Shuttle mission to the International Space Station (ISS) flown by Space Shuttle Discovery. Discovery lifted off on 9 December 2006 at 20:47:35 EST. A previous launch attempt on December 7, had been cancelled due to cloud cover. It was the first night launch of a space shuttle since STS-113 in November 2002.

The mission is also referred to as ISS-12A.1 by the ISS program. The main goals of the mission were delivery and attachment of the International Space Station's P5 truss segment, a major rewiring of the station's power system, and exchange of ISS Expedition 14 personnel. The shuttle landed at 17:32 EST on 22 December 2006 at Kennedy Space Centre 98 minutes off schedule due to unfavourable weather conditions. This mission was particularly notable to Sweden, being the first spaceflight of a Scandinavian astronaut (Christer Fuglesang).

STS-116 was the final scheduled space shuttle launch from Pad 39B as NASA reconfigured it for Ares I launches. The only remaining use of Pad 39B by the shuttle was as a reserve for the STS-400 Launch on Need Mission to rescue the crew of STS-125, the final Hubble Space Telescope servicing mission, if their shuttle became damaged.

After STS-116, Discovery entered a period of maintenance. Its next mission was STS-120 starting on October 23, 2007.

As planned, STS-116 was to be launched on 14 December 2006. But on November 29, 2006, NASA acknowledged the launch team to aim a launch on December 7, 2006, instead of the stipulated date of December 14. The launch window for the STS-116 mission opened on 7 December and extended through December 17. The seven-member flight crew arrived for launch at Kennedy's Shuttle Landing Facility on December 3, 2006 in the afternoon.

As planned, STS-116 was to be launched on 14 December 2006. But on November 29, 2006, NASA acknowledged the launch team to aim a launch on December 7, 2006, instead of the stipulated date of December 14. The launch window for the STS-116 mission opened on 7 December and extended through December 17."

Discovery was rolled over to the Vehicle Assembly Building (VAB) on 31 October. Later on, on November 1, in order to mate with the external tank and solid rocket boosters the obiter was raised into a vertical orientation and moved into High Bay 3. Rollout to Launch Complex 39B was completed on Thursday November 11.

The scientists have planned the launch the shuttle as ordered. The fundamental pay loads that are required for the 13-day mission were the P5 integrated truss segment, SPACEHAB single logistics module, and an integrated cargo carrier.

It was the 20th shuttle flight to the station. On November 16 the payloads for the mission, i.e., the SPACEHAB module and the P5 truss, were loaded from the payload canister into Discovery's payload bay and the payload bay doors were sealed. Further the external fuel tank was filled with fuel. With the completion of the Flight Readiness Review on November 28 - 29 (which evaluated all activities and elements necessary for the safe and successful performance of the shuttle during the mission, including the Obiter itself, the payload and flight crew), Discovery was given her Certificate of Flight Readiness.

After the Columbia disaster, NASA had made certain regulations prohibiting a night launch. They imposed rules emphasising the launch at the day time so that there is sufficient lights for the cameras to take pictures and observe falling debris. With the redesign of shuttle tank foam having minimised the amount of falling debris and the availability of in-orbit inspection procedures, the daylight-launch requirement was relaxed.

On November 13, the crew for the mission arrived at Kennedy Space Centre for their final four-day prelaunch training required for the mission. The pre-launch activities included familiarisation activities, rehearsal of emergency procedures and practice on NASA's Shuttle Training Aircraft. It also included a simulated countdown, which took place on the morning of 16 November 2006. Later, the astronauts went to the Johnson Space Centre in Houston, Texas and returned to the Kennedy space centre four days prior to the stipulated launch date, i.e., December 3, 2006.

After all the evaluation, the launch date was officially set to December 7, 2006, and the mission was officially given the "Go" for launch.

Whacky was the Wake Up Calls...Music on Space

Music always formed an indispensible part of our life. In Space missions too, music had its own special place. Right from the days of Gemini, a certain tradition of playing music was followed. Mission crews are played a special musical track at the start of each day in space. These tracks are specially chosen and are basically related to an individual member of the crew or is something related to their daily activity. The tracks are usually chosen by their family. During the Mission STS-116 also the music tracks initiated the day of the Astronauts.

- ✓ **Day 2:** "Here Comes the Sun" by The Beatles; played for Commander Mark Polansky. MP3 WAV
- ✓ **Day 3:** "Beep Beep" by Louis Prima; played for Sunita Williams. MP3 WAV
- ✓ **Day 4:** "Waterloo" by ABBA; played for Christer Fuglesang. MP3 WAV

- ✓ **Day 5:** "Suavemente" by Elvis Crespo; played for Joan Higginbotham. MP3 WAV
- ✓ **Day 6:** "Under Pressure" by Queen and David Bowie; played for Robert Curbeam. MP3 WAV
- ✓ **Day 7:** "Low Rider" by War; played for William Oefelein. MP3 WAV
- ✓ **Day 8:** "Fanfare for the Common Man" by Aaron Copland performed by the London Philharmonic; played for Nicholas Patrick. MP3 WAV
- ✓ **Day 9:** "Blue Danube Waltz" by Johann Strauss performed by the Vienna Philharmonic; played for Christer Fuglesang. MP3 WAV
- ✓ **Day 10:** On day 10 "Good Vibrations"; by The Beach Boys was played for the entire Discovery crew. Chosen as part of the EVA involved shaking the solar array. The track was used as a wakeup call on STS-85 when a Microgravity Vibration Isolation Mount was being tested. Curbeam was a mission specialist on that flight. It was his first trip into space. MP3 WAV
- ✓ **Day 11:** "Zamboni" by Gear Daddies; played for Pilot William Oefelein. MP3 WAV
- ✓ **Day 12:** "Say You'll Be Mine" by Christopher Cross; played for returning Expedition 14 crewmember Thomas Reiter. MP3 WAV
- ✓ **Day 13:** "The Road Less Travelled" by Joe Sample; played for Joan Higginbotham. MP3 WAV
- ✓ **Day 14:** "Home for the Holidays" by Perry Como; played for the entire Discovery crew. MP3 WAV

Mission Timeline STS 116

December 7 ....attempt 1

The pre launch preparations were over. A low cloud ceiling was announced on the night of the launch. That is why all eyes were set on the Florida skies. All throughout Florida people kept their fingers crossed.

The seven astronauts were already on board – loaded into Discovery ready for the scheduled launch at 21:37 EST. All expected a break in the clouds, but as the scheduled launch time approached it became apparent that the cloud would not break, and the launch attempt was scrubbed. The next launch attempt was scheduled for December 9, 2006. Prior to the initial attempt on 7 December, NASA had determined that they would not attempt a launch on Friday because of a cold front moving in that eventually scrubbed Thursday's launch attempt.

Launching of Discovery – December 9

December 9, 8.47 pm EST (01:47 UTC) – Discovery lifted off successfully lighting the coastline of Florida. Weather conditions – in particular crosswinds at the launch and landing sites—continued to trend positively in the hours approaching the launch window Saturday night. The fuelling process for Discovery's external tanks began at 12:46 EST (17:46 UTC) and was completed at approximately 15:45 EST (20:45 UTC).

As night launch was prohibited after the Columbia disaster this was the first night launch in the last four years. The launch was the third shuttle mission in five months after STS 121 in July and STS-115 in September.

10 December – Flight Day 2

Flight day 2 began at 15:47 UTC. The work to be accomplished this day was a thorough inspection of the Shuttle. Nicholas Patrick inspected the leading edge of the wings and the nose cap with the help of sensors and cameras attached to a fifty-foot boom. The fifty foot boom was connected to a fifty-foot robotic arm. The process took almost five and a half hours. However Patrick had to order the arm to manually grab the boom because it suffered a minor glitch. In the mean time the crew inspected the upper surface of the obiter. The astronauts also completed a check of the spacesuits to be used during the mission and prepared for docking with the International Space Station.

The Docking Day—11 December

It was 15:18 UTC. The astronauts are all prepared to dock at the International Space Station. Following the rendezvous pitch the docking to the ISS occurred ar 22:12 UTC. At 23:54 the hatch between Discovery and the ISS are opened. The crew in the ISS and the Shuttle took a detailed inspection of the obiter and unloaded the P5 truss segment of the payload bay, handing it off successfully from the shuttle robotic arm to the station arm.

On the other hand astronauts Robert Curbbeam and Christer Fuglesang ended their day entering the airlock for a “campout” sleep session to prepare for the EVA. They purged their bodies of nitrogen at a low pressure environment. This is done to avoid decompression sickness. Now the astronauts are all prepared for the fourth day EVA.

The EVA 1—Day

At about 15:47 the day of the astronauts began on the flight day 4. The day was scheduled for the first EVA. On this day the astronauts of the STS-116 added the P5 Truss segment in the ISS.

It was 20:31 UTC, when the EVA began and Curbeam and Fuglesang removed launch restraints from the P5 truss and Mission Specialist Joan Higginbotham made use of the station's robotic arm (the Canadarm2) to move the truss segment to within inches of its new position on the P4 truss. After that in order to finalize the attachment of the truss was completed the space walkers guided Higginbotham with visual cues. Then, after completing the P5's attachment, Curbeam and Fuglesang finalized the installation with power, data and heater cable connections. They also replaced a faulty video camera attached to the S1 truss. As they worked ahead of the time-line, the two astronauts were also able to complete some get-ahead tasks.

On this very day after completion of the Spacewalk, astronaut congratulated Dr John C. Mather and other Nobel Prize winners. Dr Mather was a scientist at NASA's Goddard Space Flight Centre in Greenbelt, Maryland. He was honoured with the Nobel Prize for his work on the big-bang theory. Christer Fuglesang also delivered a short speech in Swedish, encouraging Swedes and others to aspire to become future astronauts. After a period of 6 hours and 36 minutes the EVA concluded at 03:07 UTC on the morning of December 13.

The mission was pacing up. Everything was going on as scheduled. From the studies, imagery and observations of the first spacewalks, the mission managers determined that the shuttle's heat shield would support a safe return to earth. They also concluded that no more detailed inspection that was scheduled earlier would be required.

In order to reconfigure and redistribute power on the station, so that the solar arrays installed during STS-115 could be used, they had to undertake three more spacewalks. Among the three space walks, one of the spacewalks was unplanned. The first step of reconfiguring the power took place on Wednesday when the port solar array on the P6 truss was retracted, which allowed the activation and rotation of the Solar Alpha Rotary Joint on the P4. The rotary joint allows the solar arrays on the P4 to track the sun.

Usually the astronauts had to sleep at protected areas in order to avoid radiation from Solar Flare eruption.

Solar Array Reorganisation

It was December 13, and already five days have passed. Flight Day 5 began at 15:21 UTC. On this day the most high-profile activity was the attempted retraction of the P6 port-side solar array. The process began at 18:28 UTC. The controllers had to redeploy the array (from about 40% retracted) due to problems with the array folding because of 'kinks' and 'billows'. Moreover, in an effort to get the arrays properly aligned and folded, there followed a series of more than 40 commands. They abandoned the retraction efforts at 00:50 UTC. Despite retraction of 14 out of 31 bays (leaving 17 bays extended) the problems that had probably caused the loss of tension in the solar array guide wires was still not solved. This was sufficient to leave the port side arrays in a safe position to commence the activation of the Solar Alpha Rotary Joint

(SARJ) at 01:00 UTC, allowing the solar arrays on the P3/P4 truss to rotate to follow the sun.

EVA 2 .. the Flight Day 6

The second session of the EVA session was done on the 6th Flight Day. In this EVA also Christer Fuglesang participated. The day for the astronauts began at 15:19 UTC. The main work of the day was to begin the rewiring work to activate the station's permanent electrical power systems so that they can use it. To allow this changeover, station controllers had to power down about half the systems on the ISS.

Bob Curbeam and Christer Fuglesang excited the Quest airlock, 30 minutes early in order to initiate the EVA2 at 19:41 UTC. AS planned the EVA No. 2 was to activate channels 2 and 3 of the four-channel electrical system. The work progressed smoothly and after about two hours into the spacewalk the first current flowed through the reconfigured system, using the power from the P4 solar arrays for the first time. The EVA was completed in exactly 5 hours, finishing at 00:41 UTC

Flight Day 7

The Day seven was slightly relaxing. The crew deed the cleaning and preparatory tasks for the next day and the proposed EVA 3. The two spacewalkers Bob Curbeam and Christer Fuglesang enjoyed some recreation and refreshments. The first Swedish astronaut Christer Fuglesang had a very memorable day today. He was interviewed by crown princess Christer Fuglesang. He also set a 20-second Frisbee world record in space and the event was broadcast live in the Swedish TV4.

On the other hand another astronaut Thomas Reiter exercised vigorously on a machine which is known to cause oscillations in the solar arrays and tried to free a stuck solar panel. However it was not successful. The mission controllers tried to find out other solutions to the solar panel folding problem so that they can enable complete retraction, including an extended or additional EVA.

EVA3

The day began at 14:48 UTC. Astronauts Bob Curbeam and Sunita Williams by now completed the rewiring on the International Space station. The EVA started at 19:25 UTC. Lot of incidents happened on this day. Astronauts Curbeam and Sunita Williams continued to work on the retraction of a sticking solar array, enabling the retraction of another six sections of the P6 array. By now only 11 "bays", or 35% left to retract. Later on, after completion of the EVA the astronauts returned to the ISS via the Quest airlock.

It was on this EVA Sunita Williams lost her digital camera. At the post-EVA press conference it was suggested that a tether got snagged and caused the camera release button to break off allowing the camera to fall out of its holder. Curbeam later said to the MCC: "We've got the bracket and the tether. Looks like the came loose, we have the screws and the bracket and the tether.

Day 9 on the ISS - Flight Deck of Discovery

It was a preparation day. The astronauts prepared for EVA 4. The thoroughly inspected their space suits and prepared them by adjusting sizes and replacing LiOH canisters. Also the crew underwent new procedures which had been developed for attempting to enable the solar array retraction. Again, in order to protect the array from coming into direct contact with sharp metallic objects various tools were coated in kapton tape. Also the Coatings of Kapton tape provide electrical insulation if they are used to manipulate the arrays during the EVA.

EVA 4

It was a rapidly planned EVA which began at 14:17 UTC. During this EVA Bob Curbeam and Christer Fuglesang embarked on an added EVA at 17:12 UTC and tried to close completely the last eleven bays of the balky P6-port Solar Array Wing. The EVA took almost 6-hour 38-minute to complete. At the end of EVA No. 4, Curbeam ranked fifth in total EVA time for US astronauts and 14th overall.

The Undocking

It was 14:47 UTC. The flight day 11 started. It was the day for undocking. The Crew members of Expedition 14 and STS 116 posed for photos and the closed the hatches between the ISS and Discovery. Undocking was complete by 22:10 UTC. The discovery did not make a full circle because of the extended EVA 4. Due to the extended mission for EVA No. 4, Discovery did not make a full circle to film and photograph ISS, but only flew slightly more than one-quarter of the way around (through ISS zenith) before its departure burn.

December 20

The Flight day 12 began for the astronauts at 12:48 UTC. Whole day the spend verifying the integrity of Discovery's heat shield and preparing for deorbit and landing on December 22, 2006 i.e., Flight day 14. On this day two satellites

Microelectromechanical System-Based PICOSAT Inspector (MEPSI) and Radar Fence Transponder (RAFT) was launched. MEPSI looks like a pair of tethered coffee-cups, and is being tested as a reconnaissance option for disabled satellites. And RAFT is a pair of 5" cubes built by the US Naval Academy which tests space radar systems and also act as data relays for mobile ground communications. As the spaceflight was extended, the shuttle was supposed to make a landing attempt on Day 14 unless all the three landing sites were "no go".

Flight Day 13

On the flight Day 13, the day of the astronauts began at 12:17 UTC. The crew of the Discovery launched the Atmospheric Neutral Density Experiment (ANDE) micro sats for the Naval Research Laboratory. ANDE is designed to measure the density and composition of the low Earth Orbit atmosphere so that it becomes helpful in predicting the movements of objects in orbit. But to great disappointment one of the satellites failed to emerge from its launch canister. ANDE approximately 30 minutes after its launch emerged from the canister.

Landing at KSC

Every launch and landing involves certain amount of risks. Therefore, every launch and landing is very carefully planned. Each and every thing is inspected thoroughly. The weather down on earth is also considered before landing. The day 14 for the astronauts began at 12:17 UTC.

The weather at both the Edwars Air Force Base and the Kennedy Space Centre were not very congenial at that day. There was high Cross winds at Edwards Air Force Base and clouds and showers at the Kennedy Space Centre Landing

Facility on the first orbit . SO it was possible that the landing would take place at the White Sands Space Harbour. Since the landing of STS-3 in 1982, it will be the first landing at White Sands Space Harbour. Had landing taken place at White Sands, it could have taken as long as 60 days to return the obiter to Kennedy Space Centre. However it did not happen so.

However, because of the unfavourable weather condition the first landing opportunity at Kennedy Space Centre was abandoned. However, at 21:00 UTC coordinates were sent to the shuttle to re-attempt a landing at Kennedy along runway 15, as the first contingency landing attempt at Edwards had been scrubbed due to high cross winds. At about 21:23, the de-orbit burn of Kennedy occurred and the landing time coincided with the local sunset time 17:32 EST (22:32 UTC). Tough it coincided with the local sunset time the shuttle landing was not considered a night landing. The official rules for a night landing are sunset + 15 minutes. Though it was not considered a night landing, they had to use the xenon runway lighting system. Discovery touched down 30 seconds before the expected time. Landing time at Kennedy was at 17:32 EST (22:32 UTC).After successful completion of the mission Discovery landed safely with all its crew members absolutely fit.

❑

History Retold the Soyuz Journey

Life moved on. Sunita was back on earth. She continued her work at the Johnson space centre where she worked as an Astronaut Officer. She also served as the deputy chief of the Astronaut office between February 2008 till October 2009. During this period she did a lot of PR work sometimes sharing her experiences to the astronauts, assisting the mission launches, etc. After landing on earth from her first space sojourn Sunita started training the backup crew for the Expedition 30 that was to go in the year 2011. She was again selected to go for the expeditions 32 and 33.

The American space programme had five space shuttles of which they are proud of. They are the Challenger, Columbia, Discovery, Endeavour and Atlantis. However its shuttle challenger met with a big tragedy in 1986 killing now six astronauts on board and one teacher McAuliffe who participated in the mission. It disintegrated within seconds of its launch. Another tragic event in the history of American Space mission was the disintegration of the SS Columbia that disintegrated killing seven promising astronauts including Indian Astronaut Kalpana Chawla in the year 2003. It was a great setback to NASA. By now America was left with the Atlantis, Endeavour and the Discovery. In 2011 the Atlantis was retired and so was Discovery in the year 2012. The Discovery was later shifted to the Smithsonian Natural History Museum. However a few months later the SS Endeavour went on his last flight marking the end of the American Space programme.

After the tragic end of the five space shuttles of America, the only option was the Russian Soyuz. That is why all the launches to the ISs were shifted to Baikonur with Soyuz as the launch vehicle.

Soyuz was unlike the Shuttle. The Shuttle that could carry seven astronauts, only three astronauts could travel in Soyuz. It was a little cramped inside but was more reliable than the shuttle. The advantage of Soyuz is that till now it has not caused any causality. It is more or less a delivery vehicle that the shuttle which could double up likes a laboratory too. Sunita Williams was selected again for the expeditions 33 and 34. Her second trip up to the ISS was aboard a Soyuz in 2012.

Sunita was back to school in Russia and undertook some intensive preparation Schedules. Since her first space journey there was lot of changes. BY now the construction of the ISS was complete and it was a fully functional laboratory orbiting the earth. With seven more interior modules, the space station is much bigger since Williams went there last. "Six people on the crew instead of three has its pluses and minus. There are more people to interact with but it is harder to get everybody together for dinner at night." Yes, the crew did find time every other week to share their favourite foods and have a "party" in space. "You eat with a spoon and you never really need a fork or knife. And you don't want to be the one who lost their spoon," says Williams, who lost her spoon one day and found it floating a module-and-a-half away, where the suction caught it. "You never take your spoon for granted ever again!"

The ISS became huge more or less like a football field with giant solar panels forming its wings, weighing over 4,00,000 kgs. It had all the modules of US, Japan, Russia and Europe. Unlike four in the earlier times, each expedition now included six astronauts

Initially the launch was scheduled on 15 July 2012 at 8.40 a.m. Baikonur time. She was to travel with Aki Hoshida of Japanese Aeronautical Agency and cosmonaut Yuri Malchenko on Expeditions 33 and 34. In June Sunita's mother visited her and so her sister Dina an Mike who joined her for launch. Before two weeks to launch Sunita with her colleague Aki and Yuri entered the last phase of preparation. They shifted from star city to Baikonur, then to the Cosmonaut Hotel where they had to pass several exams and a week of quarantine.

Williams was launched from the Baikonur Cosmodrome in Kazakhstan, along with Russian Soyuz commander Yuri Malenchenko and Flight Engineer Akihiko Hoshide of the Japan Aerospace Exploration Agency, on July 14, 2012. They were welcomed on the International Space Station on July 17, 2012, by NASA Flight Engineer Joe Acaba and Russian cosmonauts, Expedition 32 commander Gennady Padalka and

Flight Engineer Sergei Revin. Williams spent four months conducting research and exploration aboard the orbiting laboratory. She landed in Kazakhstan on November 18, 2012, after spending 127 days in space.

"I've been here 18 years," said Williams. "I've only gone up twice." "On the second mission, the bulk of the mission was science experiments," she said. During that 2012 mission, she did three spacewalks and performed a schedule of experiments for elementary schools, colleges, universities, companies and private investors. They did hundreds of experiments, all while maintaining the space station. The crew spent the majority of the time doing science experiments and EVAs but they also clicked a lot of pictures. "The Cupolá is such a wonderful place. Even when you don't want to take pictures anymore, you want to hang out and look out of the window. Your eyes open to more and more things when you are up there longer. You see not only the artistic ways in which the earth looks but also how it is changing. It feels like it's not just the people there but the earth is alive itself," she adds.

Williams works with Extravehicular Mobility Unit (EMU) spacesuit hardware in the Quest airlock of the International Space Station

During their expedition, Williams and Hoshide performed three spacewalks to replace a component that relays power from the space station's solar arrays to its systems, and repair an ammonia leak on a station radiator. With 50 hours and 40 minutes, Williams once again holds the record for total cumulative spacewalk time by a female astronaut. In addition, Williams, who has spent a total of 322 days in space on two missions, now ranks sixth on the all time US endurance list, and second all time for a female astronaut.

While everything is time lined, that timeline can change depending on what needs to be done to the space station. "The hardware needs some maintenance, care and love every now and then to make sure it is working," said Williams.

Sunita enjoyed the Soyuz. She wrote about it on her blog, "There is food water and toilet. It was all Russian food: Cans of meat and fish, Cheese Cookies and Juice in little juice boxes. It was like camping. We slept a lot, ate our food and used the toilet. Of course we chatted and laughed. Luckily Dina bought me a Sudoku Book so I ripped out a couple pages, put them in my flight books and did a few puzzles in my free time." The launch took eight minutes but it took two days to dock at the ISS.

Once Again in the ISS...

The International Space Station has a representative name. It is an international project involving more than a dozen nations and some inspirational cooperation between the American and Russian governments. When Williams went on the ISS for the first time in 2006, both the American Space Shuttle and the Russian Soyuz spacecraft had been shuttling astronauts to the ISS since 1998.

There is a three-person crew aboard the International Space Station, unless the Soyuz is docked to it. Since 2011, when NASA ended the Space Shuttle program, the Soyuz is the only way to get to and from the ISS. "The whole reason we have a space station is that we have an international space station," she said. "These are countries that sometimes didn't get along, trading engineering methodologies. There's a huge diplomatic plus that comes out of this kind of work."

It is not simple, it's hard," she said. Each country came with "a different set of principles and values and motivations, and were somehow able to put all that aside and build this laboratory."

On the other hand, she said, "It's not so hard when you are up in space. You are a team. You've got to help each other." In some ways, the astronauts in the space station take on a healthy "us against them" mentality, said Williams.

As she reached the ISS, Sergei Revin, Gennady Padalka and Joe Acaba were already there. With Gennaldy as the Commander, when Sunita and Aki arrived the ISS, the six member crew was all set for the Expedition 32. The ISS now has a living room, kitchen, bathroom, bedroom, toilet, closets, offices and even a home gym unlike the ISS that Sunita visited last time. However the bedroom actually is a sleeping station on the walls, floor and ceiling where each station has a sleeping bag and space for some personal items and a computer. They all gathered in the living room where they had their breakfast and dinner. It is basicallu one of the modules. The kitchen is the store house of packets of dehydrated food packets and the bonus containers with the favourite food of the astronauts which was brought aboard by the carriers. You cannot cook in the kitchen. The toilets are somewhat same as that of the toilets at earth but there is a tube for urine and potty. The urine is filtered and recycled for water and the toilet wastes become trash. The trash is being loaded on the return vehicles in every two or three months. Most of the trash burns on the way when the vehicle enters the atmosphere.

Life inside the ISS requires a lot of adjustments. Being from different nationalities its is all the more difficult to live in a close confinement. However when you have to be trapped together, you have no option but to be mature. In April, a Soyuz arrived to bring the other two to Earth, and to drop off two different astronauts. They were both Russian. She thought, "I have some heavy responsibility here." he felt the responsibility with the two new Russian crew members to be something of a diplomat. Now, she refers to them as "like two of my brothers, the Soyuz guys."

The offices are the place where the main work on the ISs happens. It is the place where most of the work for which the space station is built is done. However everyone was fond of the Cuppola—which is an observatory with seven windows offering the best view of the Earth, Space and the ISS itself. Everyone liked to sit in the window seat. By now the ISS is about a million pounds in weight and is as long as a football field about 375 feet with an acre of solar panels that powered it. It also had a fifty-five feet long giant robotic arm that could lift up to 220 pounds and eight solar array. The modules Zarya, Zvezda, Destiny, Unity and Quest formed its vital modules. Apart from that, there was the European Lab Columbus, Kibo that belonged to Japan and the mini research module the Cuppola, Rassvelt . The storage module Leonardo was also an indispensible part of the ISS.

The Transition of the ISS

Many changes occurred in the ISS by 2012. Sunita talks about the food in the ISS, "food could potentially be one of those expedition – triggering issues—something that gets people mad at each other—so being semi-conscious about all this is important". The choice of food, menu, etc. all evolved down the years and nowadays the containers are used within nine days. The opened several containers containing a whole range of food, such as beverages fruit, meat, eggs, snacks, bread etc. The astronauts choose food on the basis of their preferences. They eat their favourite first and then the least loved ones. Sunita says, “You ever save something because the other guys will eat it and then you will go mad. So just eat what you like and then we end up eating the ones we don’t like thereby exhausting everything.” It was actually funny to ponder over the food.

As always the day at ISS begins with the wake up music calls in the PA system at about 6 am in the morning. By 8 pm they wind up the work and by 10 pm the lights are out. At the weekends it is usual cleaning and communicating with friends and family. Sometimes they even have a movie show or games.

As earlier, exercises formed a vital part of the mission. Sunita exercised as usual just after her arrival at the ISS. They had the old CEVIS and the new machine ARED or the Advanced Resistive Exercise Device on which she spend most of her time. The ARED provides weights and resistance allowing the workout required for a microgravity environment. Since there is no gravity in the ISS the calcium in the bones get redistributed and muscles also begin to break down. That is why a certain amount of work out on a regular basis is necessary for the astronauts to deal with the risk of losing bone density and muscle mass.

Olympic Games..Falmouth Road Race and Nautica Malibu Trithalion

It was during her second space mission, there on earth the Olympic games was going on. Every evening, the astronauts would sit together to watch the special moments of the game from NASA. Sunita who was an athlete at heart planned her races on space. The upcoming event was the 7.2 mile Falmouth Road race. Sunita decided to participate along with her sister Dina and her friends. She discussed about it with her parents over the video conferencing. Her number was emailed to her and next morning she eagerly waited for the race to begin but due to rains in Flamouth the race was delayed. When the sky was clear, Sunita started running at her TREAMIS. And within one hour and three minutes and fifty-two seconds, Sunita completed her race. Another race she participated during her stay at the space was the Nautica Malibu Triathlon which was rather difficult than the marathon. It was a8 km swim which Sunita did on the ARED then a 29 km on CEVIS and a 6.4 Km race which she did on the TREAMIS. It took Sunita about one hour forty-eight minutes and thirty three seconds. She was happy. Though it was a tiring job she was pleased to complete the race.

Above everything, it was the EVA that mattered. Her preparations started in Early August as her scheduled space walk with Aki was on the 30th. She readied her space suit, charged the batteries and checked thoroughly. She reviewed the tasks they would do during EVA and almost all their discussions circled around what if some adversities happen during EVA and how to handle those situations. As Sunita comments, Even planning when to go to the space and what to eat are important. Remember you are in a suit eight hours for a six hours EVA.....". However, Sunita followed her own customs and traditions before going for an EVA. She ate Fluffernutters—wheat bread sandwiches with peanut butter and her favourite marshmellowcream, fluff and Tvoreg—a Russian delicacy.

In this spacewalk Sunita and Aki are assigned to install a Main BUS switching Unit and a camera on the robotic arm. As they came across a sticky Bolt, and after ten hours long space walk, Aki and Sunita returned to the ISS to plan out another EVA which they scheduled in the same week. This time the space walk was successful. They fixed the Main Bus switching unit and the camera on the robotic arm. This time the EVA was successful and Sunita already held a record of prolonged stay on the space. She spent almost fifty hours and forty minutes which was the longest duration any woman would. She overruled Peggy Whitson who spends hours in space.

Experiments on ISS

The crew in the Expedition 32 performed almost 201 investigations, including blood cells testing, analysis of human hair exposed to long duration space flight and extreme weather observation. Sunita remained busy collecting samples everyday and send it to the earth. They collected urine, blood, saliva, stool etc., every day and send them to earth for analysis.

Apart from that they undertook several other experiments from biology to Physiology. All these experiments continued till Expedition 32. Sunita watched the Hurricane Sandy and wrote, "Hurricane Sandy and the Franken storm are covering up everything from the Chicago area to past the east coast from our vantage point. Now we can see the Swirls... I hope Dad has Gorby tied down so he doesn't blow away."

While on this mission Sunita also received biological payload of two spiders and several fruit flies (For the Spiders).

The two spiders Cleopatra and Nefertiti—were sent up to the Space for the experiment. Now how did they select these particular spiders? There is a long story. In the year 2011-12 the children were asked to submit Microgravity experiment. The winners of 14—16 category was Sara Ma and Dorothy Chen from Michigan. Their theme of experiment was "Could Alien Superbugs Cure Diseases on Earth?" In order to test this they have send up Bascilius Subtilis to observe if the strain of bacteria growing in the microgravity environment is more infectious than the other bacteria's that grows on Earth? In the other category i.e the 17—18 age group was Amr Mohammad of Egypt whose theme of the experiment was, "Can you teach an old spider new tricks?" It was his zebra spiders that were named Cleopatra and Nefertiti. The main aim of the experiment was to see if the spiders could survive in the new atmosphere and catch their prey in a state of weightlessness. They wanted to study whether the state of weightlessness will affect their ability to jump over their prey and how would they adapt to the new environment. Cleopatra and Nefertiti spend more than ninety days in the ISS and the experiment showed that they were comfortable in the new environment.

Sunita was attached to the two Spiders. She became emotional about their fare well. She packed them in for the return trip in the boxes and gave a hug before she placed them in the Dragon SPACEX Capsule. She wrote, "I hope they make it . Little Cleo is being elusive again. Big dark Titi is in the corner…not moving much. I will be happy to pack them up—hopefully it isn't like I am putting them in a coffin….hang in there, there are many fruit flies on earth…and no, we Don't have bugs up here to my knowledge. …May be bedbugs but nothing floating/flying around the open so releasing them here would not be a good idea." Sunita was actually very worried about the spiders whether they would be able to make it to the earth. However, Cleo died on the touchdown but Nefertiti survived. Later she was taken to the Smithsonian Museum and was put on display.

Apart from the biological experiments Sunita also undertook some other investigative projects which are quite interesting. One among them was the Meteron where she remotely drove a robot that was in Germany. This experiment was done to check out how an astronaut would control a robot from an orbiting spacecraft. Usually robots are used for Mars missions. So it was necessary to observe and analysis how an astronaut would control a robot from a moving spacecraft that orbits round the planet. Using robots is much more convenient than sending astronauts to unknown places in the space. Sunita operated the Lego Mindstrom on Land and was successful in managing tasks through it.

The days at the ISS passed with so many experiments, maintenance work and public relation events. Often they would conference with their family in the weekends. On earth Dina arranged the calls for their parents with her sister up above. Many of Sunita's friends had the opportunity to speak with her. She also had a conversation with her favourite teacher from middle school MS Dinapoli.

Birthdays and Celebrations

The crew abroad the ISS had certain moments of celebrations too. It was 13 September, the crew dug around the service module. With chocolate-covered espresso beans, dates, oysters and chocolate pudding, they had a great party time. It was Gorby's birthday. Sunita's stuffed Gorby was brought out and everyone had an enjoyable time.

Another event they celebrated abroad the ISS was the birth day of Sunita Williams on September 19. She recollects, "It was a great day—no not a day off—but a great day to take a couple of minutes look out of the window, check out our awesome planet which is home to so many species that couldn't live anywhere else, and think all the cake ad ice-cream i have had in the past, on this day. It makes me smile just thinking about it!" Now on this birthday only Aki and Yuri were on board with her. Joe and Sergei had already returned to earth, so she had to celebrate her birthday only with Aki and Yuri. Sunita's birthday also coincides with the Annual Pirates Day. Therefore Aki, Yuri and Sunita all dressed up as pirates and they had dressed in bandanas and eyrpactches. She talked to her family on earth who had a cake for her. Sunita blowed the candle virtually and they celebrated her birthday with some of her favourite food, including saag, paneer, lobstar and yakotari. Yakatori is a Japanese dish skewered bacon or pork in sauce and good luck Japanese beans and rice.

She recalls, I cannot think of a better place than the ISS to spend a Birthday. She wrote It was a great day—no not a day off—but a great day to take a couple of minutes, look out of the window, check out our awesome planet which is home to many species that could not live anywhere else, and think about all the cake and ice cream I have had in the past, on this day. It makes me smile just thinking about that."

Apart from that they celebrated the Indian independence day on August 15 and Diwali. They raised the tricolour and thanked everyone for their prayers and support.

Socialising in the ISS was somewhat unusual—you have astronauts of different countries and sometimes it is boring because there are no cinema halls or malls to linger around. However they had very little time to get bored because they undertake so many experiments and activities that keeps them busy. Yaki, Yuri and Suni all three had enough to keep themselves going. However the bonding between the astronauts is remarkable. In one interview Sunita told, "I went down to the Russian end of the station to just ask Yuri a question and I found myself there for over an hour and a half. We just had so much to talk about for the next couple of week's activities, exercise philosophies, the new crew and the landing process, families, friends, rumours at home, news, the origin of names, etc. We had each other cracking up... I did find Aki a little later in a remote part of the Japanese segment practising his Ukulele."

In another incident on the ISS, she remembered being unable to deal with the thought of walking.

"You just always float. There was a module that struck down from the ISS and I would float by it every day. One day, I thought if I had to walk, I'd have to be very careful and jump. I just couldn't get my head around how it would be to walk there because I had been floating for so long," she said.

Safe Return to Earth....

It was time to come home. On November 19, after a long 125 days Sunita, Aki and Yuri dressed up and floated over to Soyuz which was docked at the ISS. They ensured everything before they could actually undock. They ensured that all things are hatched properly and the journey would take another few moments.

It was an exciting moment for them. After successful completion it was their turn to return home. They became emotional, wanting to be at home touching the earth, swimming in the ocean, lake and pool. They missed a shower or bath on earth.. their families and so. And landings and launching always involved certain amount of risks. Every mission has risks and uncertainties.

However her second mission was quite comfortable because Soyuz was known to be more reliable. The Soyuz comprised of three parts—an orbital module, a descent module and a propulsion module. The astronauts usually are strapped to their seats at the propulsion module. The two modules propulsion and the orbital modules are detached from the capsule to burn when they re-enter the atmosphere. As the capsule reaches the atmosphere the exterior starts heating up. As it plummet towards earth at a very high speed, therefore within the module there are controls for the astronauts to navigate. Before fifteen minutes of landing four parachutes are made ready and the rate of descent is decreased gradually. Among the four parachutes the bigger one is visible because it carries the astronauts to earth.

The seats inside the module are lined with soak absorbers in order to cushion the landing. However landing is s slightly bumpy ride all the same. The Astronauts now feel heaviness on their head and their arms no longer floats. This feeling actually acknowledges their homecoming and their reaching the earth from a zero gravity area to gravity. Their head seems to weigh so much that it becomes almost impossible to stand up.

Sunita and her crew landed on Kazakhstan. When they reached earth they remained seated in their seats for some time because the search and rescue team was yet to be reach and also to avoid the blades interfering the parachutes. Sometimes the search and the rescue team take a while to reach the spot. When Sunita and her team returned it was quite cold. Despite severe winter's cold night people eagerly awaited and cheered their safe return. The team rescued three astronauts and Yuri, Aki and Sunita was safely landed after successful completion of their mission.

They were then taken to Baikonur and then to Russia. Coping up with the earth's gravity was quite difficult. It took a few more days to adjust with the gravitational atmosphere. Sunita flew to meet her family at Houston. Her sister Dina, Parents and her pet Gorby came to greet her. She was overjoyed and came out of the Airship with unsteady steps on earth.

On Reaching Back

Sunita was made for the space. She was happy on her safe landing but at the same time she missed the ISS desperately. The four months at the space passed very soon. She said," It was a sad day for us, somewhat bittersweet, when we got back." She missed ISS and the space. But she could do something of her choice on earth which she couldn't so in the space, i.e., enjoy a pizza.

The astronauts take several weeks to recover from microgravity effects. Their health is monitored. They spend time in briefing the activities done on the ISS and also a few PR activities. Almost six months they spend of Public relation activities. Sunita was fortunate to have the privilege of being related to two nations. After her return from the two missions she was warmly welcomed by India as well as Slovenia.

She visited India and Slovenia and also several places in the United States. She visited several schools, including Needham and Falmouth. She was quite energetic but six month PR activities were actually tiring. Her father Deepak Pandya accompanied her in most of her journeys. Each time he saw his daughter he was amazed to see the kind of vigour she possessed. She replied to all questions she is asked by children and adults when she visited them. She feels that it is a great opportunity to communicate with people but it is more exhausting than being in the Space.

In 2013, Sunita visited India again where she was again flooded with questions like how to become an astronaut, her experiences, how is to be in the space, about NASA programmes, and a lot more. She enthusiastically shared her story with all those who asked. She then went to Slovenia to meet her mother's relatives. There the president of Slovenia conferred a decoration on her for her contribution to the promotion of natural sciences and for being the role model of the young Slovenians. She was the hero for the young generation.

However Suni was very fond of Kalpana Chawla, another astronaut of Indian descent. Like her, Sunita also stressed on the breaking of borders. She believed in the unifying nature of space programmes. It is really appreciable to bring together the people across the borders to work in tandem to build up the space station. All astronauts irrespective of their country worked together for a common goal. Stressing the internationalism displayed in the space programmes, Sunita said, "I think it is a role model programme for many other international programmes on ground…My own personal feeling is that when you leave the planet, you leave as a human being. You are the citizens of earth.

When she is not in space, she is the deputy chief of the commercial crew branch of the Astronaut Office. NASA is working with Space X and Boeing as those companies develop a commercial spacecraft to go to the ISS. Space X is expected to fly in 2017, and Boeing in 2018.

❑

Other Than a Professional Astronaut

Gorby ....Love for Pets...

Sunita Williams often described herself as a strong believer of the Hindu god Ganesha. She carried the Bhagwad Gita along with her during her space journey.

Sunita Williams is also fond of dogs. Her pet a Jack Russell Terrier named Gorby is her constant companion who has participated with her in the famous television show the Dog Whisperer on the National Geographic channel on November 12, 2010.

Gorby was Sunita's love, life and everything. There was none other than Gorby that coule make her happy. She was very possessive bout her Jack Russel Terrier. Throughout her space sojourn Sunita kept in contact with her family through video chat or calls. But the one she missed most was her pet Gorby. Sunita and Michael already had Turbo, a Labrador retreiever when she brought little pup Gorby home in 2001. Since she was at Russia she was highly impressed by the President Mikhail Gorbachov. President Gorbachov brought about several democratic reforms in Russia. Sunita named her pet after him as Gorby.

Gorby was very close to Sunita's heart. She took him along to all the places she travelled. But while she had set for the launch of Discovery, she could not carry Gorby along. However Gorby was a spectator of the launch programme. She carried a little stuffed Gorby to the ISS to give her company. Often in her speeches she mentioned Gorby. Gorby thus became popular among every one. Flat Gorby was the name given to his picture after a children's book character named Flat Stanley. On earth Sunita's colleagues at NASA kept pictures of Gorby at their offices and computers. A sort of Gorbymania was looming around the astronaut circle. Further when a team of astronauts went for the underwater NEEMO mission their mascot was the Flat Gorby. NASA send a huge fridge magmet of flat Gorby as the mascot. When Sunita went on the ISS mission Gorby went to live with her parents in Boston.

When their children were settled the Pandya family moved from Needham to Falmouth. Her father worked and did his research in the university and her brother Jay was in Navy for several years. Later on he went to pursue his degree on Nuclear Technology. Her sister Dina finished her college studies at Smith and did her MBA from Babson College, Massachusetts. She joined Woods Hole

Oceanographic Institute in Woods Hole, Ma. Sunita got daily updates of Gorby from her sister Dina. Her Husband Michael who was in the Navy left his job and went to train himself in law enforcement. He joined as a federal officer and travelled across the country. Later he settled at Houston.

After returning from the ISS, Sunita involved herself in a lot of PR work. She travelled to India and Slovenia to share her experiences.

In September 2007, Williams visited India. It was her third visit to India. She was warmly welcomed by the people of Gujarat. She went to Ahmedabad where her extended family was overjoyed to receive her. She went to the Sabarmati Ashram and her ancestral village Jhulasan in Gujarat. She spoke to students in Ahmadabad and Mumbai, and she met the then Indian President Pratibha Devi Singh Patil. She spoke at the International Astronautically Congress in Hyderabad. On October 4, 2007, Williams spoke at the American Embassy School, and then met Manmohan Singh, the then Prime Minister of India.

The Prime Minister announced Sunita Williams Scholarships for Higher Education during her stay in India. She is the first person of Indian descent(but not an Indian citizen) to be awarded with the Sardar Vallabhbhai Patel Vishwa Pratibha Award by the World Gujarati Society. In the years that followed many commendations and awards came her way. ABC Television named him the Person of the Week. She was given a honorary doctorate degree by the Colby College. The Indian government conferred her Padma Bhushan, making her the first non-Indian citizen to receive it. She also received the Navy Commendation Medal for her contribution to the field. She became a well-known personality worldwide. With her NASA trademark uniform by this time she had become a favourite among not only the kids but also the grownups as well.

She continued her work at the Astronaut Office at the Johnson Space Centre. She also held the position of the Deputy Chief of the astronaut office during February 2008 till October 2009. She also worked as an astronaut trainer and assisted astronauts by sharing her experiences. She represented several NASA mission launches during this period.

Her Passion...

Sunita is very fond of running, swimming, biking, triathlons, windsurfing, snowboarding and bow hunting. Sunita joined society of Experimental as a Test Pilot and Society of flight Test Engineers and American Helicopter Association. She made a grand performance in all of these.

She achieved Navy Commendation Medals two times, Navy and Marine Corporation Achievement Medal and Humanitarian Service Medal and various other service awards.

Sunita Williams, Expedition Fourteen flight engineer, participated in the mission's third planned session of extravehicular activity (EVA) as construction resumes on the International Space Station. Astronaut Robert Cur beam STS- 116 Mission specialist also participated in the 7 hour, 31 minutes space walk. During the training in NASA she developed the skills in technical briefings Physiological training and preparing for T-38 flight training, as well as learning water and wilderness survival techniques.

The Blogger Sunita..

Throughout her missions Sunita maintained her personal blog. She was a poet at heart. She was on the ISS on January 1, 2007. The New Year is always a special day for everyone. The crew in the ISS were also very excited. They saw the full moon behind them from the ISS. She made a poetic entry of this day on the space station's log book:

We look out of the window and realise we are almost humans to heaven

We look at the earth and it's not hard to believe

What those billions of folks down there can achieve

Our thoughts wander to the explorers of the past

So many hardships and sacrifices to make the moulds they cast.

The fruit of their labour is that we sail a ship of golden solar arrays

Along a path that is constant and stays

Today's achievement is a result of cooperation and friendship around the worlds

The faces, the language, the flags—all swirled

Like so many others before us, we dedicate our lives

In hopes that the future of Humanity thrives

Here's to future generation of explorers, you are our motivation

To continue to explore as one combined nation.

An Indian by Heart

Sunita Williams, though born and brought up in America, she was very much an Indian at heart. She loved Indian food and also appreciated Indian ideologies. Her father inculcated in her the Gandhian ideology of simple living and high thinking. Father Deepak Pandya and mother Bonnie, both were great family makers. Deepak Pandya always valued Indian culture he tried to imbibe those values in his children too. It was from them Sunita and her siblings learned what family bonding means, how to live in an organised way and importance of friends and family.

All the members of the Pandya family epitomised Indian values and customs all throughout their living. As her parents sum up Sunita – she learned perseverance from her brother Jay, her husband taught her the importance of love, respect and friendship and of course her fellow competitors in school days helped her to develop a competitive attitude and importance of team work, dedication and healthy living. Her career in the Naval Academy imbibed in her the capability of surviving in an male dominated atmosphere. She also learned some of the practical skills like underwater survival.

Everyone close to her influenced her and taught her one thing or the other. To prepare oneself as an astronaut is not an easy task. Sunita enhanced her learning from all experiences she gained from everything she came across. Her Russel Jack Terrier, Gorby taught her humour and companionship.

India was in their body and mind. Bonnie recollects, "Deepak was fond of making sukhadi and pakora. We helped him by cutting vegetables for the pakora and brown sugar for the sukhadi." Often the family ate pakoras and sukhadi made by Deepak Pandya on the weekends. They listened to Indian music and Sunita with her brother and sister would enjoy having a meal sitting on the floor in Indian style. They ate with their hands—a rare thing done by American children.

The Pandya family visited India several times. Sunita came to India in 1998 as a small child and after the Columbia Crash. People in her village are proud of her. The entire Mehsana district prayed for her safety while she was abroad ISS. A Rally was also organised at her ancestral village Julhason. She watched Indian movies and enjoyed them. They visited places like Rajasthan, Delhi, Ajanta, Ellora, Madras, Bangalore, Bombay and Shabarmati Ashram, Porobandar in Saurashtra, Gujarat. Deepak Pandya explained the children about Gandhiji and non-violence and what Gandhi meant to the Indians. Sunita was impressed by Gandhian ideologies of truth, non-violence and love. She also practises simple living and high thinking.

In one of her visits to India in India she went on a camel ride and later she insisted on her parents taking the camel back home. She loved Indian music and sang songs such as Ichak dana, Ichak Dana....kabhi kabhi, etc., when she was a small girl.

Often Sunita declares herself as a committed devotee of Ganesha. When she was launched to the International Space Station (ISS) with STS-116, aboard the Space Shuttle Discovery, on December 9, 2006, to join the expedition 14 crew, among the personal items that Sunita carried to the ISS, were a copy of the Bhagavad Gita, a small figurine of the Hindu deity Ganesha, and some samosas.

Like all girls, Sunita was her father's child too. Her love for her father was immense. While undertaking the space expedition she carried a letter written in Hindi by her father Deepak Pandya too along with her other favourite items.

Indians around the world got a special Diwali message from outer space as Indian-American astronaut Sunita Williams sent out warm wishes on the occasion from the International Space Station. Williams along with Yuri Malenchenko of Russia and Japan's Akihiko Hoshide left for the ISS aboard a Russian spacecraft on July 15, 2012. Floating upside down in the space station as she appeared on the screen before the Indian tricolour for a local TV show, Williams said, "I just want to wish everybody in India and people of Indian origin around the world a happy Diwali".

She spoke to Indian-origin student of New York University Riti Bhalla, who as a city-based TV host interviewed Williams on her Diwali special programme, the tricolour was not the only Indian object accompanying Williams in space. She has also carried a picture of the Sanskrit word 'Om' and a copy of the Upanishads, which her father gave to her before she left for the space mission.

"I did bring some things that have to do with India from my father, particularly a peaceful 'Om' that stays outside my crew quarters where I sleep and the Upanishads so I can read it while I am up here. "It is a small version (of the Upanishads) but it definitely brings the wisdom to us while we are here and allows us to think of the true meaning of life and what we are doing". In August, 2012, she had displayed the tricolour on board the International Space Station and wished Indians on the eve of their 66th Independence Day.

All these show how passionate she was about her country of origin.

❑

All Usual and Unusual – All in Space

"Pre-breathe and getting ready to go outside...it is a long process. We are up around 08:30 and get outside around noon. We work outside for 6-7 hours and then go through an hour process to get out of the suit. Misha was instrumental in getting us all suited up. He was working away for all three EVAs to get us ready."

The suit they wore was specially designed. They wore long underwear which had tubes of cooling water through it for their heat regulation.

Have you ever imagined how it could be to smell in space? Often these topics like smell of the space, feel of the space etc., were some of the things people were very eager to know. Sunita said that after coming in from EVA, they would get a metallic smell. All the space suits, tools and airlock, etc smelled like metals. This they thought may be because all the things in the space station are basically made of aluminium. They realised that they really get a weird smell and sort of like burning metal, which is distinct and also repeatable. Sunita Said, "The first time I smelled it was after Beamer's and Christer's first EVA on STS-116. It was overwhelming when we opened that hatch and the smell migrated into the Station. You can still smell that burning metal smell in the space suit a couple of days after. It lingers in the fabric when you take a whiff. So we also decided that there is really no smell in space—it only smells because we are operating in close proximity to something that is ionizing."

How about the feel of space, often people questioned Sunita Williams about how it is to be in space. You can of course work upside down, right side up, sideways - anyway you want to, to make it convenient. In Sunita's words" We train in a very large pool, called the Neutral Buoyancy Laboratory, for these spacewalks because floating in the water column helps us simulate the weightlessness of space. With the help of the divers we can float at a certain depth in the water and practice our tasks. However, gravity is still there so we still have a sense of up and down. Plus the pool walls give you the sense of right, left, forward and aft in your periphery vision." As you know there is no gravity out in space and also there are no walls. That is why the astronauts could not feel what exactly is the feeling of up or down, forward and aft left and right at all.

Williams once said "This is good and bad. Good because it allows you to manoeuvre yourself with your arms and hands in any direction to put your worksite right in front of you.

Bad, because if you change your orientation from what you practised and are familiar with, potentially at night when it is really dark out there, your sense of direction may need some help. Really knowing the layout of the outside of Station and using visual landmarks such as antennas and cameras, etc., are essential for orientation. Space is absolutely a 3-D world in comparison to our 2-D world on Earth."

This is what Sunita has to tell us about the sound in space "I thought I would talk about this one a little, reflecting on my experience from my EVA on STS-116. What is true and what most folks think is that there is no sound in space. From almost all recollections I would agree. However, during the solar array retract attempt during the Shuttle mission, I "heard" something. If you remember, Beamer and I were up on the mast canister of the solar array we tried to retract. The folks inside and on the ground were sending commands to the motor in the canister to retract the array. My hand was holding onto a handrail on the canister. As soon as that motor started turning, I "heard" it. Actually, I heard it through my arm, connected to my hand, connected to the structure of the canister, connected to the motor assembly. It was so natural for me to think I heard it - I forgot I was in space and there is no sound in space. In fact it was the vibration—which sound is—that generated the "sound" I heard, which so closely resembled the motor. Acoustics - so cool!"

❑

Reminiscences of the ISS

Locks of Love......

Their expeditions were full of excitement. Along with the seriousness involved with the expedition there was a lot of fun filled moments during their stay.

By mid February 2009, she completed almost three spacewalks from the ISS with her fellow astronaut Michael López-Alegría. During one of these walks, a camera became untethered, probably because the attaching device failed, and floated off to space before Williams could react. There were certain lighter moments. Williams performed her first extra-vehicular activity on the eighth day of the STS-116 mission

An interesting event during their stay at the space was Sunita William's hair cut. After launching abroad, Sunita Williams got her hair cut by one of her fellow astronaut

Higginbotham at the International Space Station. Her pony tail was brought back to Earth by the crew of STS-116. She donated her pony tail to Locks of Love.

Boston Marathon.......

Williams became the first person to run the Boston Marathon from the space station on April 16, 2007

Mother Bonnie Pandya recollects...her tiny little one saying " *I want to run"* . The same passion and determination was seen when she decided to participate in the Boston Marathon from space.

Sunita was determined, energetic and diligent. She participated in the Boston Marathon by running 42.2 km (26.2 miles) on the Space station's treadmill—a rare activity any one could dream of.

Her job involved more than the spacewalks and the heating system. She reached out to her passion and participated in the Boston Marathon. While on earth she had run the Houston Marathon and qualified for the Boston Marathon with a record of three hours twenty nine minutes and fifty-seven seconds. She did not want to give up because she felt it was an honour to qualify for the Boston Marathon. Her sister Dina too participated for the Marathon. The Boston Athletic Association Sent her an official runner's bib—No 14,000. Almost 23,000 people participated in the race. Her sister Dina completed the Marathon on Earth along with the NASA astronaut Karen Nyberg.

The whole day was scheduled but she did get time to train for and then participate in, while in space, the Boston Marathon. "I qualified for it and I didn't want to waste my qualification," said Williams. Running while floating, she said, is painful. "You have a harness pulling you down."

It was raining in Boston but inside ISS it was calm and quiet because most of the six member crew was sleeping when the race started. Sunita with her Navy blue T shirt was all set to start the race. With a goal to complete 42.2 km, she tethered herself to the TREAMIS and started. A few minutes after the race started, the people at the ground control said humorously, "We estimate you've completed your Marathon right now…" the ISS ravels 7.7 km per second and in less than six minutes it covers that distance. The ground staff cheered on, played music and kept her updated about the race on ground through the radio. Oleg woke up and came over to Sunita. He had oranges with him and he kept them ready for Sunita. Running on the TREAMIS was laborious. It puts lot of strain on the legs. Sunita took several breaks to massage her legs and drank water. He kept pace with her speed and in four hours and twenty-four minutes, she completed the Marathon run. It was 6.23 GMT when she radioed her message to the Ground control. " I am done…" she was overjoyed. She celebrated her completion of race with a post-race feast—curried vegetables with peanuts and chicken with peanut sauce. She actually travelled 121,600 kilometres, i.e. almost thrice round the world.

She talks about the meal she had during the race. Pre-race meal included lasagna and ravioli. They too had pesto paste and sundried tomato paste. During the run, She took about 6 bags of water and had REAL oranges. She recollects, "The Expedition 15 people brought us some fresh fruit so we had blood oranges up here. Oleg cut some up and was throwing them at me as I ran. It was so nice to taste a real orange. It has been some time now since we had fresh fruit. Yummy!"

The post-race meal comprised curry vegetables with peanuts, chicken with peanut sauce.

Sunita followed a fixed exercise schedule. It included 20 minutes biking, 1 mile walk, 4 miles running, 3.6 miles run/walk and then she took a break. After the break they went for a 35 minutes biking, 5 miles running and spend more time on the resistive exercise device (RED) this week at lower weights, primarily to stretch out her legs.

About her running the Marathon, She said, "A lot of people do things with kids," she said. She has worked extensively with children, and the running the marathon was "a good way to highlight that even astronauts have to work out." As an astronaut, PR, such as talking to Cape Cod Wave, is part of the job. But a bigger part is the reach-out and education.

Wasabi – Her Foe

In the vacuum of space, staring out of the window of the ISS can take up hours of an astronaut's time. A 24-hour period has 16 sunrises and sunsets on the ISS. On her 2007 mission, Ms. Williams ended up having to contend with a formidable foe – wasabi. In early March 2007, she received a tube of wasabi in a Progress spacecraft resupply mission in response to her request for more spicy food. When she opened the tube, which was packaged at one atmospheric pressure, the gel-like paste was forced out in the lower pressure of the ISS. In the free-fall environment, the spicy geyser was difficult to contain. The spicy Japanese condiment was going to be the highlight of an otherwise bland meal, when the mismatch of the pressure led the jar to explode.

Ganesha and the Bhagavad Gita

Sunita was interviewed by Ajith Balakrishnan of Rediff.com while still in flight, and by quite a few others, including Dilip Sardesai and school children from Singhania Education Centre when she visited India shortly after the visit. When boarding for her historic flight, she said she carried a copy of the Bhagavat Gita, a small statue of Ganesha and some samosas. Later she ordered some more spicy food from the ground. I am repeating that not with any particular pride – but that is what she is said to have carried. Though not India-born, and only partly of Indian blood, she obviously loved things Indian.

Cleaning the Loo

How amazing it would be to clean the loo. The urine containers had to be emptied in the thrash and send as thrash at the Progress vehicle. Misha thought that only experienced people did this. But Sunita was confident that she knew how the system operates. Misha could not believe that she is experienced enough for this work. Sunita was eager to learn. Misha taught her and asked her to swear not to tell anyone about the whole affair. He pulled almost seven urine tanks later. Sunita Says, I realised he had pulled a Tom Sawyer on me.

Conversation with the Dog Whisperer Cesar Milan

Staying in the space is pretty monotonous. She missed her near and dear ones—especially Gorby. She missed Mike and her parents too. Gorby also sensed her absence because he could only hear her but not smell or feel, all these days. Sunita was also desperately missing her pet. SO when she had a chat with Cesar Milan, popularly known as the Dog Whisperer, she tried to collect all information about managing her dog and how Gorby could be helped to cope up when Sunita is away for so long. She was actually very happy to talk to the dog whisperer.

I Have My Mother's Green Thumb...

Sunita was very excited when she saw the soybeans that sprouted in the microgravity environment. She wrote, "I have my mother's green thumb'. Among numerous experiments the astronauts also experimented on how plants thrive in microgravity environment.

The Celebrity on TV

Sunita and LA had an interview with the celebrity talk show hostess Martha Steward. She interviewed her for the show where her sister Dina also joined as an audience. Sunita and LA showed the soybean plants they are growing in the ISS. Martha also asked her about tips on making their meals appetising in the ISS.

Meeting Her Highness

One fine Day the crew of Expedition 15 were asked to dress up in their finest Suits. Suni, Oleg and Fyodor wore their official best and waited eagerly. It was for the scheduled visit of the British queen to the NASA"s Goddard Space Flight Centre in Maryland. The queen arrived on time and the conversation started. The queen could witness a rare view of Sunita's hair flying upwards, and the microphones flying between the astronauts. She had an amazing view of the ISS and talking to the astronauts. She keenly listened to the experiences in ISS that the astronauts shared with her. It was indeed a fascinating experience.

The Alvin Episode

Swimming and diving always attracted Sunita. Alvin was a submersible owned by Woods hole Oceanographic Institute, MA., where Sunita's sister Dina worked. This is a vehicle used for underwater assignments. Sunita had the experience of conversing via the sea to space phone connections miles away. She talked to Tim Shanks who was working on Alvin two miles below the sea and Sunita in the Space 200 miles above on the ISS.

Sunita and Tim shared a fifteen minute conversation on January 27, 2007 through radio. Sunita and Tim talked about aliens they have seen in two extreme environments. Sunita said, "We haven't seen anything up here, but I am sure you've seen stuff that looks pretty unnatural down in the sea". Tim Shanks replied, "yes Suni, some of the life forms down here looks like aliens. We are both living life in extremes.'

At times they became status conscious and asks each other about exchanging their positions. The desired to switch their jobs and so their conversation encompassed so many things related to their work and environment.

They talked about their work and had a good time chatting till they signed off.

Her Three Iconic Spacewalks in Nine Days

By the end of the mission's ninth day Sunita has completed three successful EVAs. 31, 2007 she and the commander of

ISS Mike Lopez ALegria spend seven hours and fifty-five minutes outside the ISS. They worked on the construction of the ISS. They tried their hands on the power and cooling systems of the ISS. Again on 4 February the went for the second EVA and the third on 8th. Towards the end of the mission on April Sunita undertook another spacewalk with the Expedition 15 team, thereby creating a record of highest number of the spacewalks by a woman. She recollects later, 'we train so much for the EVAs that we Don't ever feel afraid. I felt like it was pretty natural to be out there first of all... when i had some free time I looked up and saw us flying over our planet. I looked further up and saw the vastness of space with the millions of stars crystal clear above me. I save the northern lights shimmering and dancing green above Earth's surface...from inside the station one can see some of this, but it was all there just in front of my vision.

During the first expedition, Sunita, after many attempts, completed a spacewalk of 32 hours and 36 minutes. In 2012, Sunita was launched from the Baikonur Commodore as a part of the Expedition 32/33. On this mission, she was accompanied by Japanese astronaut Aki Hoshide and Russian cosmonaut Yuri Malechenko. the Arkalyk in Kazhakhstan. Till November 2012, Sunita made seven spacewalks in a total time of 50 hours and 40 minutes. The holds the fifth position among the world's experience spacewalkers.

Tea Breaks...Language and ...Attributes

While talking about the first week of their life in the ISS, Sunita Williams says that It has been a crazy and emotional week. Lots going on to get the Expedition 14 crew and Charles ready to go home. It seems like everyone had something to do at the last minute. Writing, cataloguing, conducting experiments, running a marathon - life has been a little crazy".

All the astronauts were busy. Fyodor and Oleg helped Charles with his experiments and Misha in preparing the Soyuz for departure. Sunita also wanted to take time off for her tea or coffee. But it took her more than 2 months to get along with the schedule. She said, "Tea" breaks were fun. Usually if you stop for tea, someone will feel the desire to join you. So, there is usually good "water cooler" conversation which seems to always end up with language."

The most interesting part of getting along was the language. The astronauts belonged to different nations and they spoke different languages. But when they spoke, words of one particular language got along with another language very well. Sunita says, "For example, "Scotch" in Russian is tape and "pampers" means diapers. That is just one type of nuance. There is also the emphasis on different syllables which makes some words sound entirely different. I couldn't stop laughing about the word hippopotamus, which was pronounced like 2 separate words, "hippo-potomus," with the emphasis on the third O. I was laughing saying how "cute" that was. Now "cute" was a word Misha picked up from me and thought was entirely funny. He would imitate me say cute - probably about Gorby because I said it/say it continuously."

Getting along with each other is very important for the astronauts. Sunita observed that after living with Misha and LA we found that they started taking on each other's characteristics. Both adopted Sunita's way of saying "too," as in "too funny," and "too much" and in the same way she picked up Misha's way of saying essentially "whatever," "da ladna" in Russian. Sunita said, "Now that Fyodor and Oleg are here to stay, I am anxious to see and learn the characteristics they will "bring to the table." The closed environment of this little ship in space is not only a technical/scientific experiment, but truly a cultural and human experience."

Cool Places They Have Flown

Patagonia! We saw this view from outside - incredible!

When they saw Australia from space it almost seems like another planet from up there. She said, "If I didn't know it, I wouldn't have thought we were flying over earth."

They were able to see the US in daylight again, especially the northern parts and glimpses of the Pacific Northwest through the clouds for the first time. They also saw some of Africa and a little of Europe.

Thought of Walking

In one incident on the ISS, she remembered being unable to deal with the thought of walking.

"You just always float. There was a module that struck down from the ISS and I would float by it every day. One day, I thought if I had to walk, I'd have to be very careful and jump. I just couldn't get my head around how it would be to walk there because I had been floating for so long," she said.

The Fools Day—April 1

Sunita loved to enjoy. Along with work she loved to have lighter moments of fun and frolic with her colleagues. One Such incident was the April Fool's Day.

Sunita Williams undertook several experiments in the biological lab at the ISS. The miniature laboratory for the first time at the ISS was named Lab on a Chip Application Development-Portable Test System or the LOCAD-PTS. The system detects presence of bacteria or fungi in the surfaces of spacecraft. It detects in a very fast rate than any other normal culturing methods.

Moreover the astronauts no longer need to send the samples to the laboratories on Earth. On March 31, 2007 Sunita assembled the components of the LOCAD-PTS and took several readings. The initial readings were taken to find out whether the instrument was functioning properly or not. On the other readings she took readings of various objects around the cabin in order to find out whether there are bacteria or not. The readings showed the presence of bacteria. The principal investigator Mr Wainwright exclaimed, "The cleaner the sample the longer the analysis takes". It is very important to detect the micro organism in the spaceships because in long space voyages it will not only help to check the health of the astronauts but also to monitor the electronic and structural materials, which can be corroded by certain fungi and bacteria.

When they took the last set of readings, it was almost midnight. Sunita Said, "Ah the last set of readings for LOCAD-PTS looks somewhat strange.' After a few seconds Sunita announced surprising her tense colleagues 'Happy April Fool's Day'. She then told them the readings were just fine.

ARISS and Standing at Nobska Light

"We have a ham radio on board. Sometimes we do ham radio sessions with groups of children," said Williams.

Most Astronauts are licensed amateur radio operators who are allowed to call sign in KD5PLB. Sunita was one among them. She had regualar conversations with the kids of different schools on Earth. The ISS and the Amateur radio is an inseparable part of NASA's Educational out each. It is popularly known as the ARISS. Sunita had several sessions with different institutions when she was in the ISS.

Once it so happened that a child on Cape Codbuilt his own little radio station on his own. His name was Dominic Fucile, a young high school student. He set up a call with Williams' sister, Dina Pandya, and they went to Nobska Lighthouse. With the ISS flying overhead, they had a five-minute window to talk. Williams was happy to do it. She said we do it o provide inspiration to the next generation. "For the kid, he was cool as a cucumber," said Williams.

"But from what I heard later, he was beside himself." Williams was sort of that way too. "It's the coolest thing to know you are talking to someone standing at Nobska Light," she said.

Usually when the ISS pass through a city or town the schools and institutions were informed beforehand, so that the operator on the earth can pick up a signal and establish contact with the astronauts in ISS. Usually they are given a ten minutes window to interact. As the schools are avare of the schedules in advance the students already have a prepared questionnaire. Sunita interacted with lot many schools during her mission in the ISS.

A squadron Safety Officer and later, an instructor at the Rotary Wing Department of the Naval Test Pilot School.

During her time in orbit, she did seven spacewalks, several science experiments, extensive robotic work, completed a marathon and triathlon, and even blogged and tweeted from space—all of this while making big decisions manning the International Space Station as commander of Expedition 33. Sunita Williams: astronaut, engineer, pilot, runner, swimmer, pet-lover, and a woman who is a role model for anyone interested in space exploration.

Nautica Malibu Triathlon

It was during her second space mission, there on earth the Olympic games was going on. Every evening, the astronauts would sit together to watch the special moments of game from NASA. Sunita who was an athlete at heart planned her races on space. The upcoming event was the 7.2 mile Falmouth Road race. Sunita decided to participate along with her sister Dina and her friends. She discussed it with her parents over the video conferencing. Her number was emailed to her and next morning she eagerly waited for the race to begin but due to the rains in Flamouth the race was delayed. When the sky was clear Sunita started running at her TREAMIS. And within one hour and three minutes and fifty-two seconds, Sunita completed her race. Another race she participated during her stay at the space was the Nautica Malibu Triathlon which was rather difficult than the marathon. It was a8 km swim which Sunita did on the ARED then a 29 km on CEVIS and a 6.4 Km race which she did on the TREAMIS. It took Sunita about one hour forty-eight minutes and thirty three seconds. She was happy. Though it was a tiring job she was happy to complete the race.

Space Food

Their food comprised canned fish or meat with cabbage, potatoes, rice or white sauce. Sunita recalls 'Peanut butter and marshmallow cream sandwich on a tortilla! Twice! One per EVA. Yummy. My ultimate is a thin spreading of peanut butter, then about ½ inch of marshmallow cream...Heaven. I carbo loaded with ravioli with meat sauce the night before the EVA. It is fine actually. We have tubes of garlic paste and pesto paste that are really nice to add to these meals. All the main dishes are slightly bland to accommodate all kinds of taste buds. So, our family and friends have supplied us with tubes or jars of sauces to spice things up. Other types of sauces which have come in handy are wasabi, horseradish, Korean hot sauce (that red stuff in the squeeze bottle). That way each of us can make the food as spicy as we want'.

After finishing 3 EVAs they had a little feast with herring in burgundy sauce (tomato sauce really), rye bread, pickles, borscht and mashed potatoes with mushrooms and onions. Sunita and Misha took a "fresh" garlic clove and followed it up with some hot tea. Though the meal was not appetising the astronauts enjoyed table chatting about the view from outside and what we had experienced.

❑

Finding the Right Balance

Now that Williams is back on Earth after four months in space, she is taking out time to do things she enjoys. "You have to make sure you don't get swallowed up in one thing," she says. "Being balanced is very important."

Williams flew to the ISS again on July 15, 2012, as part of the crew of Soyuz TMA-05M. She was a flight engineer on Expedition 32, and on September 16 she became commander of Expedition 33. She made three more space walks, totalling more than 21 hours, retaining her space walk record with a total time outside the ISS between her two flights of more than 50 hours. She also completed a triathlon in orbit by using a treadmill, a stationary bicycle, and a weightlifting machine to simulate the swimming portion of the race. Williams returned to Earth on November 11 after nearly 127 days in space. Her two spaceflights combined lasted more than 321 days, making her second, after American astronaut Peggy Whitson, for the most time spent in space by a woman.

In 2015, Sunita Williams is among four astronauts who have been selected by NASA for commercial flights to the International Space Station (ISS) from US soil. Williams, Robert Behnken, Eric Boe and Douglas Hurley will be trained for commercial spaceflights that will return American launches to US soil and further open up low-earth orbit transportation to the private sector, the US space agency said. They will work closely with company-led teams to understand their designs and operations as they finalise their Boeing CST-100 and Space Crew Dragon spacecraft and operational strategies.

"Congratulations to Bob, Eric, Doug and Sunita and welcome to the Commercial Crew team," noted John Elbon, Boeing vice president. "We look forward to working with such a highly-skilled and experienced group of NASA astronauts as we carve a path forward to launch in 2017."

"These distinguished, veteran astronauts are blazing a new trail – that will one day land them in the history books and Americans on the surface of Mars," said NASA administrator Charles Bolden.

Sunita Williams was a US Navy captain, became a helicopter pilot, logging more than 3,000 flight hours in more than 30 different aircraft and an astronaut who has spent a total of 322 days in space and currently holds the record for total cumulative spacewalk time by a female astronaut (50 hours and 40 minutes). She ranks the sixth on the all-time US endurance list and second all-time for a female astronaut. No doubt she has won accolades in her life. But balancing the professional life and personal life was not an easy task. She agrees, however, that balancing a demanding science career and family is challenging for women. "You can do both. It's hard but it can be done," says Williams. "I am married but I don't have children. I have two dogs and my family and friends help me out with them. They are not kids but they are something you have to be responsible for. If you are going to pursue this career, you need to have a solid infrastructure to help you out with things."

With her head in the stars and feet on the ground, Williams is an inspiration to all women in science. Her advice to women considering a career in space is, "Don't put limits on yourself and don't let anyone put limits on you. Find the thing you like to do because when you like something you do it well." Prospects for women in space are huge, she adds. "We have done equally as much as the men have done. I think in the short amount of time that women have been flying, we are contributors, counterparts, and partners to the men who are doing all this sort of stuff."

While everything is time lined, that timeline can change depending on what needs to be done to the space station. "The hardware needs some maintenance, care and love every now and then to make sure it's working," said Williams.

When she is not in space, she is the deputy chief of the commercial crew branch of the Astronaut Office. NASA is working with Space X and Boeing as those companies develop a commercial spacecraft to go to the ISS. Space X is expected to fly in 2017, and Boeing in 2018.

For space exploration in the future, Williams believes it is just a matter of time before humans get to Mars. "We think robots can pave the way for us but we have to take the other steps in the meantime. That's why we have the international space station to test out some of that stuff. It is an engineering project. Everything in engineering is done stepwise and we find out where the pros and cons of each step are and we capitalise on that."

Sunita is a lady of firm decision, continuous perseverance and struggle. Why we find her inspiring is because she followed her heart and achieved her dreams, no matter how tough it was. She took up an offbeat career when not many women aspired during those days. She believed in making the most of the opportunity, having run a marathon in space she proved that when you have will, you have the way.

❑

Ladies Extraordinaire

Women and space do not often go together. Today women are walking hand in hand with man in every field. They explore every possible thing and of course they do not leave space behind.

The journey to space dates back to the 1960s. Different countries have sent their woman astronauts to the space. Russia was already much ahead of other countries in the run. Most women in space have been United States citizens, primarily with missions on the Space Shuttle. Three countries maintain active space programs that include women: China, Russia, and the United States of America. In addition, a number of other countries - Canada, France, India, Iran, Italy, Japan, South Korea, and the United Kingdom - have sent women into orbit or space on Russian or US missions.

Women in space encounter many of the same challenges faced by men: physical difficulties from non-earth conditions and psychological stresses of isolation and separation. Scientific studies on female amphibians and non-human mammals generally show no adverse effect from short space missions, although the effect of extended space travel on female reproduction is not known.

Russian Woman in Space

Valentina Tereshkova, was the inaugurator who created history as the first woman to go to space in the year 1963. Valentina Tereshkova was a Russian cosmonaut who was launched with the Vostok 6 Mission on June 16, 1963.

The first woman to walk in space was also a cosmonaut: Svetlana Savitskaya was on her second mission when she spaced-walked on July 17, 1984. Russian Yelena V. Kondakova became the first woman to travel for both the Soyuz programme and the Space Shuttle. Yelena Serova became the first female Russian cosmonaut to visit the International Space Station on September 26, 2014.

The space programme of Russia even hosted international cosmonauts. Some of the international cosmonauts hosted by Russia include, Helen Sharman from the United Kingdom (1991), Claudie Haigneré from France (1996 and 2001), Anousheh Ansari from Iran (2006), Yi So-yeon of South Korea (2008) and Samantha Cristoforetti from Italy (2014) and six American women have entered space as part of the Soyuz programme.

Woman from the United States

The space programmes of the United States also initiated some of the most successful space missions with woman as a part of it. However until 1983 they have not sent a woman to space. Sally Ride was launched with the seventh Space Shuttle mission in the year 1983. Since then more than 40 American women have entered space and served in several space Shuttle flights from 1983 to 2010.

It was Sunita Williams who made the Americans proud by creating a record of maximum space walks in space. is an American astronaut and United States Navy officer of Indian-Slovenian descent. She holds the records for total spacewalks by a woman (seven)[2] and most spacewalk time for a woman (50 hours, 40 minutes).[3][4] Williams was assigned to the International Space Station as a member of Expedition 14 and Expedition 15. In 2012, she served as a flight engineer on Expedition 32 and then commander of Expedition 33.

Like Russia, the US, rockets have launched international astronauts too. Prominent among them were Roberta Bondar and Julie Payette from Canada (in 1992 and 1999/2009), Kalpana Chawla of India (1997 and 2003), and Chiaki Mukai and Naoko Yamazaki of Japan (1994/1998 and 2010) who flew as part of the US space programme.

Women not only worked as a part of the space missions in the US but also a number of high profile women have contributed to interest in space programmes. Lori Garver initiated a project called, "AstroMom" to increase the visibility and viability of commercial spaceflight. She aimed to fill an unused Soyuz seat bound for the International Space Station because "...creating a space faring civilization was one of the most important things we could do in our lifetime."

Chinese Ladies in Space

After Russia and the US, China had send their woman astronaut to space in the year 2012. It became the fourth nation to send women into space, after Russia, the former Soviet Union, and the United States. In 2010, China selected their first female astronaut from among the married mothers who were from the ranks of fighter pilot. They preferred married women because the Chinese thought that married women were "more physically and psychologically mature". Also they took into consideration of the fact that there may be some unknown effect of spaceflight on women. However, the director of the China Astronaut Centre has stated that marriage is a preference but not a strict limitation. China's first woman astronaut, Liu Yang, was married but had no children at the time of her flight in June 2012.

Mothers in Orbit

Motherhood makes complete women. Isn't it a different experience to see a mother in Space? So many mothers have travelled to space and created and recreated history. The Saga continues. And now there are many more to come.

During 1986 the topic of "mothers in space" was a topic of common discussion in every coffee house. Especially when the Space Shuttle Challenger exploded less than 2 minutes after launch with the loss of all the crew. One of the crew, Christa McAuliffe, was a wife and mother of two. One way the disaster is linked to motherhood in space is that McAuliffe's mother had supported her dreams to be the first teacher in space, and she noted that although her daughter had trained for any number of emergencies on the Shuttle, no one had anticipated a disaster of that scope. Another astronaut Laurel Clark was an astronaut mother who died in the Space Shuttle Columbia disaster, leaving behind her husband and son.

Shannon Lucid was questioned by the press at that time on how her children would handle her being a mother in space. She was already a mother when selected in 1978 to be an astronaut. She went on to set an American record for time spent in space. During her 188-day stay in space, she sent daily emails to keep in touch with her family.

However many mothers went into space. Anna Fisher became the first when she flew into orbit aboard Discovery with mission STS-51-A on November 8, 1984. Valentina Tereshkova was the first female in space to become a mother (after her flight). The first French woman in space was Claudie Haigneré, in 1996. She is married to Jean-Pierre Haigneré (also an astronaut), and is a mother of three, with one from that marriage.

Some more recent examples include astronaut and mother Nicole Stott, who made history in 2009 when she sent live Twitter messages from the ISS. Karen Nyberg became the 50th woman in space in 2008, and she is has logged more than 340 hours on long-term missions in space. Cady Coleman spent Mother's day in orbit in 2011. Human mothers in space face a number of challenges related to managing family life and spaceflight. By the 2010s, email and Internet phones were noted as being used for communication with families when separated. One mother in space maintained a more tangible connection with her husband and son while in orbit, by talking to them over a phone and having a video conference once a week. According to *The New York Times*, another space mother brought her son's toys into orbit.

Sunita Williams has spent more than two days or about 50 hours conducting the very tough space walks. While she makes regular phone calls from space to her husband, she says she cannot decide if she misses her dog more.

Asked if she has a choice and could take either her husband or her dog on a MARS mission, Ms Williams said, "That is an interesting choice. My dog would age quicker so I am not sure that would be a good idea. But I would get into an argument with my husband so I am not sure, I am still thinking about it."

❑

Quotes by Sunita Williams

Some Inspiring Lines by Sunita

Records are there for breaking," "It's just another way to let people know how far we have advanced. I am hoping the next generation of space explorers will just get out there and break them."

When she visited Gujarat – "I feel like I'm at home. And I hope one day one of these smiles will go to space one day," said Williams.

In democracy, change is slow but good.

Do not complain if you don't vote

★★★

Can't rule out possibility of life elsewhere.

★★★

Williams fondly recalled taking a copy of Bhagavad Gita and an idol of Lord Ganesha along with her to the space station and took tense moments in her stride. "I knew Ganesha was looking after me," she said.

★★★

"I wasn't a triple A student. I failed two college courses. But I learned from the failure."

★★★

Don't get bogged by the notions of limits, there aren't any.

★★★

"My space expedition has changed my perspective towards people. Looking down at the earth, we could not see borders or people with different nationalities. It was then that realisation dawned on us that all of us are a group of human beings and citizens of the universe," said Sunita Williams, during an event at the National Science Centre, New Delhi.

★★★

"We need an astronaut with a medical background. In my space journey I felt vulnerable because we did not have anyone with a medical background. When we make that big trip to Mars we would need a doctor on board."

The astronaut said today's generation was more open-minded and technology-savvy than she was at that age. "I wish I was 20 years younger and started my career all over again. I am envious of them."

I didn't feel as if I was a person from the United States, I felt like I was fortunate enough to be a person from earth.

Don't let anyone tell you, 'You can't do it.' That's the biggest thing — I had one squad commander [tell me]: 'Being an astronaut is for jet pilots, not for helicopter pilots.' If you know that's what you want, you've just got to go for it. You do the best you can do at what you're doing, and find out what you need to do to get into this field."

"Enjoy what you are doing, you will naturally do well at it, and if [the opportunity to be an astronaut] comes up, it is just a bonus."

❑

Acronyms Used in the Book

ARED	: Advanced Resistive Exercise Device
CEVIS	: Cycle Ergometer Vibration Isolation System
ESA	: European Space Agency
EVA	: Extravehicular Activity
ISS	: International Space Station
LA	: Michael López-Alegría
MA	: Massachusetts
NASA	: National Aeronautics and Space Administration
LOCAD-PTS	: Lab on a Chip Application Development-Portable Test System

NEEMO: Extreme environments mission operations

RED: resistive exercise device

STS: Space Transportation System

USNA: United States Naval Academy

❑

Sunita Williams – At a Glance

Bio data

Name	: Sunita Lyn "Suni" Williams
Date of Birth	: September 19, 1965
Place of Birth	: Euclid, Ohio, United States
Father's Name	: Deepak Pandya
Mother's Name	: Bonnie Pandya
Husband's Name	: Michael J. Williams
Siblings	: Jay Thomas, Dina Anna
Pets	: Gorby and Baily
Interests	: Swimming, snowboarding, bow hunting, baseball, marathons, Triathlons

Education : Needham High School (1983)

BS in Physical Sciences, USNA (1987)

MS in Engineering Management, Florida Institute of Technology (1995)

Certifications : Naval Aviator (1989), Basic Diving Officer (1988), Test Pilot (1993)

Career : American Astronaut, Safety officer at Naval Test Pilot, US Naval officer, Flight Instructor.

Awards :

- Navy Commendation Medal
- Navy and Marine Corps Achievement Medal
- Humanitarian Service Medal
- National Defence Service Medal
- NASA Spaceflight Medal
- Medal "For Merit in Space Exploration", Government of Russia (2011)
- Padma Bhushan, Government of India (2008)
- Honorary Doctorate, Gujarat Technological University (2013)
- Golden Order for Merits, Government of Slovenia (2013)

Organisations: Society of Experimental Test Pilots, Society of Flight Test Engineers, American Helicopter Association.

Space Missions: Expedition 32, STS-116, Expedition 33, Soyuz TMA-05M, Expedition 15, STS-117, Expedition 14

Fan Mail Address:

Sunita Williams

NASA-JSC

Astronaut Office

Mail Code CB

2101 NASA Rd. 1

Houston, TX 77058

USA

Address Information:

NASA-JSC

(US Space Agency)

Astronaut Office

Mail Code CB

2101 NASA Rd. 1

Houston, TX 77058

USA

Phone: (202) 358-0001

Fax: (202) 358-3469

NASA experience: Selected by NASA in June 1998, she reported for training in August 1998. Astronaut Candidate Training included orientation briefings and tours, numerous scientific and technical briefings, intensive instruction in Shuttle and International Space Station systems, physiological training and ground school to prepare for T-38 flight training, as well as learning water and wilderness survival techniques. Following a period of training and evaluation, Williams worked in Moscow with the Russian Space Agency on the Russian contribution to the International Space Station and with the first Expedition Crew to the ISS. Williams has worked within the Robotics branch on the ISS Robotic Arm and the follow on Special Purpose Dexterous Manipulator. And was a crewmember on NEEMO2 living underwater in the Aquarius habitat for 9 days.

In a Nutshell: Timeline...Achievements and Activities

- ✓ Born on September 19, 1965, Ohio, Euclid
- ✓ Sunita Williams first space experience was with the STS 116 launched by the International Space Station. She went aboard the Discovery in 2006 to join crew members on Expedition 14.
- ✓ During the expedition, Sunita, after many attempts, completed a spacewalk of 32 hours and 36 minutes.
- ✓ In 2007, she also ran the first marathon by a person in orbit, which she completed in four hours and 24 minutes.
- ✓ In April 2007, Sunita was brought back to the Earth aboard the Atlantis, during which she broke the record for single spaceflight by a woman.
- ✓ In 2012, Sunita was launched from the Baikonur Commodore as a part of the Expedition 32/33. On this mission, she was accompanied by Japanese

astronaut Aki Hoshide and Russian cosmonaut Yuri Malechenko.

- ✓ The Arkalyk in Kazhakhstan.
- ✓ Till November 2012, Sunita made seven spacewalks in a total time of 50 hours and 40 minutes.
- ✓ The holds the fifth position among the world's experienced spacewalkers.
- ✓ In 2007, Sunita Williams visited India and paid visits to the Sabarmati Ashram and her paternal village in Jhulasan.
- ✓ She is also the first person of Indian origin but not of Indian citizenship to be awarded the Sardar Vallabbhai Patel Vishwa Pratibha Award conferred by the World Gujarati Society.
- ✓ She holds several records for the highest number of spacewalks by a woman, the longest spaceflight time by a woman and the maximum spacewalk time by a woman.

❑